W0010988

NINE MONTHS TO SAVE THEIR MARRIAGE

ANNIE WEST

MILLS & BOON

This one is dedicated to my lovely friend
Anna Campbell, with fond memories of our retreat.
I loved watching whales from the balcony
while discussing how to make things difficult
for our characters. There should be more of it!

PROLOGUE

'I WENT INTO this with my eyes open, Bess, and there *are* compensations.'

Bess watched her old friend admire her diamond bracelet, her other hand smoothing the shantung silk of her designer dress.

Lara caught her eye. 'Not just clothes and jewellery, sweetie. I might be at George's beck and call, but when he's away I can please myself what I do, like catching up with you.' She leaned close. 'It really is good to see you. It's been too long.'

'It has. Jack and I have been travelling a lot.' Bess smiled as if continually hopping from one city to another, instead of putting down roots and making a life in one place, was what she wanted.

'You always were good company.' Lara pouted. 'George and I go everywhere, but when it's just me... People are small-minded. I'm not accepted in a lot of homes.'

Bess wasn't surprised. Since Lara had become a rich man's mistress, society wives didn't trust her. If Lara could hook one wealthy tycoon, she could hook another.

'They're nervous. No-one dazzles quite like you.'

'Thanks, sweetie. I try.' Lara flashed the grin Bess had first seen in the classroom, but her expression sobered as she surveyed the Eiffel Tower view over the rooftops.

'You're not completely happy?' Bess asked.

Lara's smile didn't reach her eyes. 'I made my bed so I'll lie in it. But sometimes I'd like what *you* have.'

'Me?'

Bess had been feeling under par. Jack was often absent on business and she was starting all over again in a new place. If they'd bought or even rented their own Paris apartment, instead of staying in a hotel, it would have been easier. Felt more like the home she craved.

Maybe it's not your accommodation that's bothering you.

Instantly she shut that voice down, as she always did.

'You and your delicious Jack. It was such a whirlwind marriage I wondered at first, but I know you, Bess. You wouldn't marry for anything but love. I'm happy you both found that. I remember how radiant you were in the wedding photos. And Jack looked like the cat who'd got the cream, obviously smitten.'

Lara lifted her cocktail and Bess followed suit, hiding shock behind her glass. Her stomach had gone into free fall at the mention of love.

Would Lara see the cracks in her façade? Guess all wasn't well in Bess's supposedly perfect marriage? Bess gulped her drink, the alcohol going straight to her head.

Or maybe it was the idea of Jack loving her.

If only.

She'd thought, hoped, he would one day. She'd believed that though he hadn't fallen instantly in love like she had, it would come in time.

She was still waiting.

'George is sweet,' Lara continued, 'but it *is* a transactional relationship. His priorities always come first. He's so used to getting his own way it doesn't occur to him to ask what *I* want to do.'

Bess was silent, thinking of her own social schedule, mapped out to meet Jack's needs. Dinner with potential investors here, events to promote his business there, charity events for networking. Each week his PA sent Bess an appointment schedule with copious background notes so she could perform her role, helping Jack access and charm the elite of European society and business.

After all, that was why he'd married her.

Lara continued, 'I hadn't realised how much time a mistress spends waiting for her man to make time for her.'

Lara expounded on the theme but Bess didn't hear. Her head buzzed and her heart pounded too high and fast.

Lara could be describing her own marriage to Jack.

The waiting. Coming second to his requirements every time. Not even being *asked* if she'd like to go out or stay home. His business ambitions took priority over their relationship, such as it was, though Jack Reilly was already an incredibly successful, wealthy man.

Oh, he could be tender and warm, thoughtful too, and when he set out to charm, which he often did, he was impossible to resist. As for intimacy...

Bess took another gulp of her cocktail to counteract the heat flushing her cheeks, thinking how very well Jack did intimacy. Just his kiss turned her knees to jelly and her brain to mush.

'Even though I've got plenty of time on my own,' Lara continued, 'it's hard to plan anything because George expects me to be ready for him at any time.'

Again, Lara could be describing Bess's life. Every time she began to settle in a city, Copenhagen, Madrid or London, Jack or his PA informed her they were moving on. There was little notice as the tentative life she'd tried to build was abandoned.

'I never dare relax in an old T-shirt or flannel pyjamas.'

Bess remembered her favourite sleep shirt. The cosy one she used to enjoy snuggling into. Jack had deplored it, preferring her to wear silk and lace, or nothing, in bed. Somewhere during their many moves she'd lost it.

'Sorry, Bess. I shouldn't complain. I've got an easy life for all that.'

Lara summoned a waiter for more drinks. Usually Bess would have stopped at one cocktail since she was attending an event later. But she was caught up in the creeping horror that pinched her nape and chilled her blood.

Jack had married her, but she might as well be his mistress.

Bess swallowed convulsively. Her throat lined with the razor-sharp shards of her broken dreams.

The truth hit like a hammer blow, cramping her lungs and smashing her already bruised heart. Her hands trembled and she put down her glass.

That carping voice, the one she usually silenced, was in her head again.

You're a trophy wife, no more than a mistress with a wedding ring.

The only difference between her and Lara was the marriage ceremony she'd attended, she with stars in her eyes and Jack with satisfaction at acquiring an asset to help his domination of the world's renewable energy market.

After eighteen months of marriage Jack was no closer to falling in love with her.

A great ache opened up inside Bess, so vast it threatened to consume her. Because she finally faced the truth she'd avoided for so long.

Her husband would never love her.

And every day spent in this one-sided marriage was slowly killing her.

CHAPTER ONE

Ten months later

BESS SLIPPED ON her sunglasses against the glare of blue sky, turquoise sea and a beach so white it looked like icing sugar. Beyond that was a tangle of greenery. Though she saw small clearings and buildings tucked beneath trees.

Taking the pilot's hand, she stepped from the seaplane and onto the pier while he got her luggage.

She'd seen some amazing places but none like this.

That she was here for a celebration and not work made it even more special. Since leaving Paris and Jack almost a year ago, she'd thrown herself into one challenge after another, delighting in the freedom to take projects that stretched her, testing her skills and bringing a satisfaction she hadn't felt in ages. Not since her marriage when she'd given up work to support her husband.

Bess drew a slow breath, pushing that thought aside. It was ancient history.

She inhaled sea air and something sweet carried on the breeze from the lush vegetation. Tropical flowers perhaps. She looked forward to exploring. She'd enjoyed her work but was ready to relax and this looked the perfect spot. Trust her cousin Freya to find such a glorious place.

'This really is paradise,' she murmured. 'Like something from a travel brochure.'

The pilot nodded as he placed her suitcase beside her. 'It sure is. Except this island's so exclusive I doubt they'd allow travel journalists.' He looked at her speculatively. 'You haven't visited before?'

She shook her head. 'I've never been to the Caribbean.'

'Well, you've chosen the best of the best. Absolute luxury and privacy, pristine surroundings and discreet service.'

The tall American smiled, his eyes crinkling at the corners, and it struck Bess that he was very handsome.

Yet he didn't make her pulse flutter as his eyes held hers. *Only one man had ever done that.*

Her heart sank as she wondered if that would always be the case. Bess made herself smile back, telling herself she was weary from travelling. One day far in the future she'd be ready for another relationship. Sometime after the divorce came through. Her smile grew strained.

'I'm stopping overnight,' he said. 'Ready for a charter at dawn tomorrow. I'm going to the bar for a drink. Maybe you'd like to join me?'

It was no good. Even if it was just a drink and a chat. Bess read the warmth in his eyes and didn't want to lead him on.

'Thanks. That's kind of you, but it's been a long trip and I need rest.'

The American nodded, his smile only a little dimmed. 'If you change your mind, you know where to find me.' He grabbed his bag from the plane as a woman in a neat skirt and polo shirt arrived, welcoming them to the island.

It turned out that Bess's excuse about needing rest hadn't been a white lie. She reached her glamorous and very private bungalow, politely refusing a guided tour and an offer to unpack her case. Alone, she slipped off her shoes and stretched out on the massive bed. She just had time to marvel at its cloud-like softness, foreign after months on a hard single mattress, before dropping into a sound sleep.

The sun had dipped low when she opened her eyes to a

ANNIE WEST

spectacular view of the beach beyond the trees. A stunning sunset painted the sky neon pink and tangerine.

The only sound was the chatter of birds and she felt a sense of well-being. She loved the testing nature of her work but it felt like a lifetime since she'd let herself be utterly still.

In the past ten months stillness meant time to think and that led to thoughts of Jack. Was it any wonder she'd worked till she dropped rather than leave herself time for regrets?

Her chest tightened. Leaving him had been the only way to keep her sanity and retrieve some self-respect. She'd made a colossal mistake, marrying him. No matter how much she cared for him. When love became a prison, making her a second-class citizen in her own life, she'd had no choice.

And if some tiny part of her still yearned for the romantic happy ever after she'd once imagined, time and distance were curing her.

She was getting over Jack. She really was.

Deliberately she focused on the view, not her fractured heart. She told herself she could learn to be slothful here. Her week's holiday was just what she needed. She couldn't keep running on empty, trying to forget the past by burying herself in work.

But first she had a celebration to attend. The dresses she'd ordered had been delivered. She just hoped they were as good as they'd looked online.

It would only be a small group celebrating tomorrow's secret elopement wedding. But since the bride was related to royalty and the groom was a crown prince, Bess wanted to look good. Freya and Michael would marry again later in the full glare of the public spotlight but this would be their real wedding, and Bess was determined not to let her cousin down.

She opened the door to an opulent dressing room and saw a splash of vibrant colour. Her breath caught.

Reaching out, she stroked the water-soft silk. Teaching in remote schools in Africa and South-East Asia had called for washable cottons, not glamour. It had been an age since she'd worn anything so beautiful.

Bess snatched her hand back at a sudden icy glissade down her spine.

Because these lovely dresses reminded her of the world she'd shared with Jack. Where she'd worn exquisite couture because that was the image he wanted her to project. He liked her to wear the best. And he enjoyed the way silk draped her body.

The glacial chill became a burn. A blaze that grew until it felt like there was an inferno inside her. The inferno Jack had always stoked, making her desperate for him.

Firming her mouth, Bess ignored her body's betraying weakness. She grabbed the scarlet dress she'd bought for tonight. It might be silk but it wasn't by a famous designer. It was pretty and worked well with her colouring but she'd chosen it because it made her happy and she could afford it from her savings.

Ignoring the marble and glass bathroom, Bess used the outdoor rain shower in the bungalow's private courtyard, fearing that if she soaked in the massive sunken tub she'd never leave.

Finally, dry, dressed and wearing a little makeup, Bess stepped into the scarlet sandals she'd ordered and turned towards the mirror.

She was relieved to see she'd chosen well. The silk skimmed her body in a good fit. She'd scooped her hair up, a habit she'd got into while living in hot places, and it complemented the halterneck dress.

Bess smiled, pleased to see she looked…good. For months she'd avoided mirrors as much as possible. In the early days her eyes had looked bruised and her mouth too tight. Now she looked fine.

And she was. Fine.

See? Time was doing its job. She was beginning to heal. Slowly but surely things were improving.

* * *

'Bess!' Freya leapt from her seat by the pool. 'I wanted to come to your bungalow but Michael said you'd been travelling forever and needed rest.'

'Michael was right. I was out for the count.'

Bess grinned and returned the hug. The years peeled away and it was like they were teenagers again, Freya arriving for the summer at Moltyn Hall or Bess visiting her cousin's home in Denmark.

Bess blinked. A reunion with Freya was the nearest thing to coming home that she could conceive. Her real home didn't feel familiar anymore. She'd only returned to Moltyn Hall once since her wedding and that had been a fleeting visit since her dad and Jillian had other priorities.

'Let me look at you.' She surveyed her cousin and what she saw thrilled her. 'I've never seen you so happy. You're positively glowing.'

Freya shrugged. 'Michael makes me feel that way. Enough even to become a royal.'

Bess knew duty could pall when love was one-sided. 'You're sure you want to take all that on?'

'It's part of who Michael is. It will be tough sometimes but I love him and he loves me.'

Bess's heart squeezed at the stars in her cousin's eyes. Of course they loved each other and together they were strong. 'You'll do it wonderfully. Michael and his people are lucky to have you.'

Her cousin flapped her hand. 'Enough of that. I want to talk about *you*. You look marvellous. Like you've just stepped from some luxury day spa instead of from the wilds of Indonesia.'

'Close. Timor Leste. About a thousand kilometres east of Bali. It's an amazing country.'

Freya drew her to a couple of padded lounge chairs. 'And you enjoyed it? I worried you'd jumped into something without realising how hard it would be.'

Bess thought of the difficulties she'd experienced. But they'd been nothing against the joy of contributing to something worthwhile, seeing the smiles and enthusiasm of her students and their families, and being welcomed so warmly.

'You're right. Nothing prepares you for the reality but it was wonderful.' Besides, it had been nowhere near as tough as leaping into marriage with a romantic notion that it would all turn out right, then facing the devastating truth that it could never be right. Bess fixed on a determined smile. 'So tell me, how did you organise an elopement? Royalty don't do that.'

Freya beamed. 'Michael's parents suggested we might want time alone before the big cathedral ceremony and all the razzmatazz. Michael's even taking me away after tomorrow's ceremony somewhere where there'll just be the two of us. Doesn't that sound like heaven?'

With the right man it would be.

Bess hadn't had a honeymoon. Though she had stayed in five-star luxury after her wedding and discovered the joys of sex with her new husband. Her pulse rose to a rackety beat. That memory, at least, hadn't tarnished.

But the rest of their time had been spent among strangers with whom Jack wanted to do business. Even their meals at celebrated, beautiful restaurants had been networking events, not romantic trysts.

'It sounds brilliant. Tell me about tonight and tomorrow. Who else is coming?'

'Oh.' Freya's face fell and she grabbed Bess's hand. 'I hope I've done the right thing. I wasn't sure, even though he's been such a wonderful, supportive friend to Michael. I worried it would be difficult for you, but he assured us you were on polite terms. Besides, Michael said nothing would stop you coming to my wedding. I was going to tell you last week but I couldn't reach you.'

Bess's chest hollowed. Freya's change from ecstatic happiness to guilt and anxiety didn't inspire confidence.

She squeezed Freya's hand. 'It's okay. After what I've faced, meeting whoever you've invited will be fine.' Though her skin prickled in warning. 'My phone died and telecommunications weren't good anyway. I thought I'd wait until after this week to get a replacement.' The idea of switching off totally had appealed. A way of avoiding press updates about her ex.

Freya leaned close. 'Just as well I've got time to warn you—'

Voices interrupted her and Bess turned as a group approached. A couple of women she recognised followed by a cluster of men, one of them Michael. He was talking to someone bringing up the rear.

'Bess,' Freya whispered. 'I need to tell you—'

Her voice was drowned by greetings as the others reached them.

Bess hardly heard them because her stunned gaze was locked on the tall, dark-haired man who stood back from the others. Hands nonchalantly in his trouser pockets, his wide-legged, broad-shouldered stance seemed casual yet was unmistakably provocative.

Cobalt blue eyes, narrowed under straight coal-dark eyebrows, met hers, and she was glad she was sitting as the earth rocked beneath her.

'Hello, Elisabeth. Long time no see,' said the one man she'd never expected to meet again.

Jack Reilly. Her husband.

CHAPTER TWO

JACK STARED DOWN at the woman he hadn't seen in almost a year, stunned at the impact of her. He'd been prepared for this meeting. He left nothing to chance. Yet still she caught him by surprise.

It took only one raking glance to discover she was more alluring than he'd let himself remember.

She wasn't the most conventionally beautiful woman he'd known but something about Elisabeth set her apart. Her newly acquired tan complemented her dark hair and emphasised the brightness of her unforgettable cognac-coloured eyes. Eyes wide with shock.

That gave him a buzz of satisfaction. After the shock she'd dealt him in Paris it was good to return the favour.

Anger and outrage at her desertion had been constant companions. They were there still, but now they were eclipsed by something more primal.

He felt it as a low pulse deep in his body, his heartbeat slowing to a ponderous beat. At the same time there was an effervescence in his blood, a tingling awareness that made him feel more alive, more vital, than during any recent business triumph.

Her slender limbs glowed golden and her deep red dress skimmed her delectable body. The way the silk fitted across her bust and the fact it was held up merely by two thin straps tied at the neck, was pure provocation.

Once she'd have dressed like that to tantalise him. She knew he enjoyed unwrapping her body before sharing the phenomenal sexual pleasure that had been the hallmark of their marriage.

But now… She hadn't known he'd be here. Had she worn that piece of silken temptation for another man?

His jaw clenched as he swiftly scanned the group. But Michael and the two other men were here with their partners, all currently engaged in conversation.

'Hello, Jack.' Elisabeth's voice was husky, trailing fire from his chest down his abdomen to his stirring groin.

He took a slow breath, revelling in the knowledge she was affected at the same visceral level. For despite her flattened mouth and pugnaciously tilted chin, her nipples budded against the rich fabric. And that hoarse note in her voice betrayed sexual awareness.

Jack's mouth curled. To his surprise she'd been a virgin when they married, which meant he was the only man who knew that betraying note in Elisabeth's voice.

A shadow darkened his vision. Unless, of course, she'd shared herself with someone else since him. An ache wrapped itself across his chest and right around his shoulder blades.

But whatever she'd been doing for the past ten months, the connection was still there between them, the desire.

He could work with that.

She got to her feet with that innate grace he'd noticed from the first. Because she felt at a disadvantage sitting? The lustrous fabric caught the light, shimmering over the lean length of her thighs and the curves of her breasts and hips.

Jack's palms prickled. He wanted to stroke her slender body, reacquaint himself with every inch, though he already knew it by heart. His need sang in his veins and tightened his flesh.

'I hadn't expected to see you here. I hadn't realised you and Michael were so close.'

Was that accusation in her tone? Yet her expression was placid so their companions would notice nothing wrong.

She'd always been excellent at projecting serenity and ease. It was one of the reasons he'd chosen her as his wife. That quality made her valuable for his networking, and after his childhood experiences of volatile emotions he'd had no interest in tying himself to a woman of extremes.

'We had a lot to do with each other during the development of a joint project. We discovered a lot in common.' Jack paused. 'You introduced us, remember?'

'I remember.' She glanced at the others and lowered her voice. 'You were eager for the connection. I'm glad to hear it paid off for your business.'

Jack stiffened. She said *business* as if it were a dirty word. Instead of the source of funds that had kept her in luxury and bailed out her father when bankruptcy loomed.

Of course he'd been interested in her social network. Elisabeth's family, despite her father's financial instability, was part of Europe's elite. Her father was an English aristocrat and her mother had been related to prestigious families and powerbrokers across multiple countries. Elisabeth's cousin Freya was related on her father's side to the Danish royal family and when Freya took up with a European prince, interested in innovative energy solutions for his country, Jack had seen a major opportunity.

'Thank you. Business is booming.' Which had been some small solace, given the disaster she'd made of their marriage. 'I'm pleased to count Michael as a friend.'

A knot formed in the centre of her forehead as if she couldn't quite believe that.

Not surprising since he didn't make friends readily. For years he'd been too driven to have time for a personal life. And he may initially have cultivated the friendship as a means of keeping an open door to Elisabeth's cousin Freya. For when

Elisabeth had walked out she'd disappeared. To Jack, used to being in control of his world, her disappearance had made him feel like he'd stepped off a precipice into thin air. It was only through Michael that he'd heard she was alive and well and somewhere far away.

He'd had no qualms about using that friendship to engineer this meeting. But Michael had understood.

'Is that really why you're here, Jack?' Elisabeth's hands went to her hips as if she didn't trust him. 'Just to support your new best friend?'

'Naturally. What other reason could I have?'

She wants you to have come here for her.

Satisfaction bloomed.

She shook her head, her eyes never leaving his. 'The Jack Reilly I know never acts out of sentiment. There's always some advantage to be had, a deal to be done or important person to meet.'

Her words bit deep. It was crazy. He made no apologies for being achievement orientated. That was why he was so incredibly successful. Yet she made that sound morally questionable.

'Bess! Let me introduce you to the others.' Freya looped her hand through Elisabeth's arm, shooting Jack a sharp look.

Typical. He'd done nothing but greet his wife. It had been Elisabeth who'd tried to needle him. But naturally Freya took her side.

Jack turned to join the group who eyed them with interest but who were too polite to ask about the status of their relationship. Even though Bess's sudden absence from the marriage had been the stuff of breathless public speculation.

He accepted a cold beer and let the conversation wash over him, taking part occasionally but not singling out Elisabeth. Time enough for that when they were alone.

He and his wife had unfinished business.

Rogue emotions, unfamiliar since boyhood, tightened his gut.

When she'd walked out on him Jack hadn't believed it. Still recuperating after severe flu, his foggy brain had been unable to take it in. Especially since she'd spent the previous five days nursing him when he'd been too ill to lift his head off the pillow. Her devotion had reminded him of the one person who'd ever loved him, his grandmother, the single stable point in his childhood.

For Elisabeth to look after him like that then run away made no sense.

Their marriage had been a stellar success. He hadn't been able to comprehend that she didn't feel the same. And when disbelief finally died it had been replaced by anger.

That she hadn't stayed to talk it through and give him a chance to persuade her into staying.

That she'd left him in the lurch to deal with the fascinated interest of his peers and the press. To deal with sympathetic looks and commiserations.

Jack wasn't used to failure.

Or to being made a laughing stock.

The party broke up around midnight. The ceremony was the next morning and Freya insisted she wanted everyone bright-eyed.

People were heading down separate paths to their villas when Jack approached Elisabeth. 'I'll walk you to your door.'

She stiffened. 'No need. I'll find my own way.'

Freya looked across, frowning. 'Bess, did you want—?'

'Nothing, Freya. I'm fine. You need some beauty sleep ready for tomorrow.'

Michael put his arm around his bride-to-be, pulling her close when she'd have gone to her cousin, and Jack inclined his head the tiniest fraction in thanks. He was impatient to be alone with his wife. The last few hours had tested his patience to the limit.

'She's very protective of you,' Jack murmured as the others moved away.

'I can look after myself.' She nodded in dismissal and turned down a path the others hadn't taken. Tiny solar lights in the gardens lit the way.

Jack waited a few seconds then fell into step behind her.

She spun around, that invitation of a dress flaring around her legs.

It struck him that, even if there'd been no lighting, if there'd only been moonlight to illuminate the scene, he'd never mistake her for any other woman. The way she stood, the curve of her breasts, the tilt of her head, were unique. Even the way she jammed her hands on her hips, a gesture he was only now becoming familiar with, was pure Elisabeth.

Jack felt a familiar punch of need. His pulse drummed faster as the ache that had sat in his belly all evening dropped to his tightening groin.

Even after months of humiliation and anger he wanted her.

'Why are you following me?'

He watched her breasts rise once, twice on swift breaths before answering. 'It's the way to my villa.'

'It is?'

He nodded. 'Mine's the last one before the point.' And hers was the one before his. They were the only two in this direction, isolated from the rest.

'I see.'

She didn't, but now wasn't the time to explain.

Elisabeth spun on her foot and walked away.

Jack had had hours to get used to being in her company again. Yet his thoughts blurred as he followed. Those high-heeled sandals turned her walk into a sexy sashay, hips undulating and pert buttocks highlighted by the gleam of low lights that burnished her dress. As for the bare back revealed by her halterneck dress, it was smooth and golden and pure temptation…

Jack's ribs tightened around his lungs and his breath grew shallow. His mouth flattened.

In ten months no other woman had made him feel this way. He'd barely noticed other women. Except the ones who'd made nuisances of themselves, trying to inveigle their way into his life with purred promises to take his mind off his failed marriage.

He recalled the stunning redhead who'd followed him into the hotel lift in Paris. As soon as they were alone she'd ripped open her coat to reveal her naked, voluptuous body. Then she'd told him in a throaty voice exactly what he could do with her, the descriptions vivid and direct.

Had he ever been the sort of man who'd be turned on by that? He'd always enjoyed sex. But standing in that mirrored lift, being offered sexual gratification in its crudest form, he'd felt nothing but revulsion.

For that he blamed Elisabeth.

It wasn't that he didn't want sex. He was a fit man in his prime. But the sweaty night-time dreams that plagued him featured only one woman, the one now tantalising him with the sway of her body and the memory of how very good they were together.

'Have you been lonely, Elisabeth?'

The words surprised him. He always thought before speaking but he hadn't planned this.

Because he didn't want to know if she'd been with someone else?

Her steps faltered and she cast a frowning look over her shoulder. Even that tugged at something inside. His wife might be poised and unflappable in public but he'd discovered her tiny frown when puzzling something out endearing.

Endearing! She hadn't been endearing when she'd abandoned him.

'I've been very busy, Jack. Working.'

Not a direct answer, but would she admit it if she'd been with someone else?

Something dark and feral bared its teeth. Jealousy? Why not? She was his wife. But it wasn't only possessiveness he experienced around Elisabeth.

He'd felt powerless, not knowing where she was, unable to track her down. That had been a first.

She'd been meticulous in her planning, not using the credit cards he'd given her or leaving an obvious trail out of Paris. Her friends had refused to reveal her whereabouts.

Her father hadn't known where she was. Nor had he seemed concerned that his daughter had disappeared, apparently satisfied with a message that she was okay.

That had angered Jack. It also made him realise that while she loved her family, Elisabeth wasn't close to them anymore, except perhaps her young half brother. Her father had been too wrapped up in some new project on the estate to miss his daughter.

'What about you?'

'Sorry?'

She shook her head. 'It doesn't matter. Of course you weren't lonely.'

Jack thought of his wide hotel bed. How empty it had felt without her. How quiet and dull his breakfasts had been. How all those networking events had dragged. Even his phenomenal business wins in the past year hadn't felt as triumphant as he'd expected.

But there was no way he'd admit that to Elisabeth.

He shrugged. 'Like you, I've been busy. Lots of people, lots of meetings and negotiations—'

'I get the idea.'

Was it imagination or did she sound disappointed? She turned as if to walk on. Instantly he reached out, needing to stop her, but pulled back before touching her. Coercion wasn't the answer.

'We need to talk, Elisabeth. Alone.'

'I don't think that's a good idea.'

'You'd rather we discussed this in front of the others tomorrow? Because we *do* need to talk.'

Bess drew a shaky breath and looked up into the face of the man she'd once believed made her whole.

He was arresting in that broad-shouldered, athletic way that seemed archetypally Australian. The low lights accentuated the planes and angles of his handsome face, revealing the strength of will that had made him a billionaire success story. His eyes glittered and her heart drummed, her feminine core softening.

Her body's response terrified her. After all this time and all that distance, all the things that had gone wrong between them, she should be immune to Jack Reilly.

Instead it felt like they were the only two people on the planet.

Bess swallowed, trying to focus on the shushing of tiny waves on the shore rather than her rampaging pulse.

'You're not afraid of me, are you?'

She heard something like shock in his tone and knew it was real. 'Of course not.'

It was herself she feared.

But he was right. They needed to talk. Her lawyers had written to his about the divorce and there'd been no response. She'd be foolish not to take this opportunity to sort that out.

'We need to clear the air, Elisabeth. You saw Freya tonight, picking up on the tension between us. You don't want her fretting about that during the ceremony, do you? Tomorrow should be about her and Michael, not us.'

Surprise made her blink up at him. He sounded so *reasonable*.

Had she spent their separation demonising him? Exaggerating the negatives and forgetting the positives?

Now she thought about it, Jack had always been reasonable. He didn't shout, bluster or demand. He thought carefully about what he wanted and how to get it. He negotiated. He was a phenomenal dealmaker.

That was how they'd come to marry. He'd offered her a deal. Money to pull her dad out of his financial hole so he didn't have to sell the estate that had been in the family for generations and in return Jack got her. Not because he was in love but because she'd be an asset as he conquered European markets.

'Elisabeth?'

Still she hesitated. But she wanted tomorrow perfect for Freya. If they could sort everything out and be on easier terms that would make all the difference to her cousin.

Besides, knowing Jack he'd be booked on the first flight out after the wedding. He never took holidays and his work schedule was brutal. He'd work on the plane as soon as he left tomorrow. This would be their only chance to talk.

'Okay. Let's talk.'

'Excellent.'

Did she imagine his eyes gleamed more brightly? His expression didn't change yet she had the impression she'd just played into his hands.

You're being paranoid.

They walked towards her bungalow but when they reached it Bess stopped, caution—or fear—feathering her spine. She didn't want Jack in her suite. She knew he'd take up all the space, not to mention his presence lingering later when she tried to sleep.

On impulse Bess turned aside, taking an unlit path towards the water. Jack followed the few metres until they reached the edge of the beach. It was breathtakingly beautiful, the stars bright in the velvety sky and the shimmer of the moon reflected on dark water.

It seemed sacrilege to mar the peace of this place with the ruin of their marriage but it had to be done. 'You haven't responded to my lawyer. Why?'

Under the trees his face was too shadowed to read but she felt the graze of his scrutiny. 'You can't really expect me to agree to a divorce without any discussion.'

Bess took a half step back, coming up against a palm tree. She anchored her hand against it.

'Discussion won't get us anywhere. We've already talked about what we want from marriage and I can't go on the way we were.'

'So you just walked out.'

Indignation warred with an undercurrent of guilt. 'It wasn't like that.'

She'd been tempted to leave Jack sooner except the night of their argument, their first and only real argument, he'd collapsed, running a high temperature as he succumbed to a virulent flu.

Yet she'd left as soon as he was well enough to care for himself. Because she was worried he might persuade her to stay if she lingered?

'It felt like that. One minute you were feeding me paracetamol and hot drinks and fussing about whether I was comfortable. The next you announced you'd had enough and left. I didn't even have the energy to follow.'

Her throat caught. 'You'd have followed me?'

She hadn't allowed herself to imagine that. It was the sort of thing a man would do if he really *cared*. Jack wasn't cruel but she'd increasingly come to realise, and he'd actually spelled it out to her, that theirs was no more than a transactional relationship. She would always be a commodity to him, an asset.

'Of course I'd have followed. You're my wife.'

The timbre of his voice was warm chocolate, lush and tempting.

He moved towards her, a creature of silver and shadow, a man so elementally attractive she felt a twist of arousal deep in her pelvis. Her nipples budded against silk as her breasts seemed to swell.

Excitement merged with despair at her instinctive reaction.

'I missed you, Elisabeth.'

He'd missed her? Bess's eyes widened.

It wasn't something she'd imagined hearing from him.

He stood so close the balmy night grew warmer from his body heat. Or perhaps from the arousal flooding her body. She swallowed hard and leaned back, palms against the trunk of the tree behind her, trying to ground herself.

'You don't believe me?'

She shook her head, not because she doubted his word but because he'd astonished her. 'I didn't think you would.'

She'd expected him to be angry. Apart from anything else, he planned everything and for her to disrupt his life would be infuriating. But she'd convinced herself that while she'd been valuable to him she was hardly indispensable. He didn't really need anyone to help him. People thronged to him, eager to be part of whatever he was involved in, and it seemed his new ventures were highly successful.

Jack's eyes locked on hers. 'Then you don't know me as well as you thought. I had investigators combing Europe, looking for you.'

Bess saw he was serious. Of course he was, he'd never lied to her. On the contrary he'd always been honest, brutally so sometimes.

'I wasn't in Europe.'

She was so stunned at the idea of him searching for her she couldn't think of anything else to say. She'd assumed he'd wash his hands of her. Especially once her lawyer contacted his about a divorce.

'So I found out, much later.'

Bess frowned. There was something in his tone she couldn't identify. Something that sounded like strong emotion. Yet for Jack their relationship wasn't about emotion. Pragmatism yes, convenience and even sex, but not emotion.

Her head whirled as she struggled to absorb what he'd said. He'd missed her, he'd actually admitted it. He'd sent people searching for her.

Excitement bubbled but she forced it down. It wasn't her, Bess, he missed. It was his well-groomed, well-connected partner, adept at softening business with hospitality and charm.

She stood taller though he still towered over her. 'Actually, Jack, I'm very tired. Let's not do this now. We can meet for breakfast.'

When it would be broad daylight and she wouldn't be so hyperaware of his physicality. Of how very much she wanted to lean against his hard, enticing frame.

For she'd missed him too. So much. And now he was so close it threatened to overwhelm her.

She couldn't handle this, couldn't trust herself. Despite knowing he could never be the man she wanted, he was the man her body craved.

Fear propelled her. Without waiting for his response, she straightened, pushing away from the tree behind her. But she miscalculated for instead of obligingly stepping backwards, Jack stayed where he was.

Her momentum made her breasts graze his torso and as she stepped forward her leg slid between his.

Bess froze, stunned. The reality of his iron-hard chest and thighs, burning with that familiar male heat, tore free something she'd tried to keep bound tight inside. She gasped, shocked at the too-familiar sensations rocketing through her, undermining every good intention.

'I have a better idea.' He inclined his head, his voice dropping to a note that turned her willpower to water. 'We sort this out now.'

'This? The divorce?'

Jack shook his head. 'No, my darling wife. *This*.' He wrapped one arm around her back, his other hand supporting her head as he leaned in and kissed her.

CHAPTER THREE

LATER BESS BLAMED the word *darling* for the way she froze.

Jack had never called her that before. He'd called her sexy or very occasionally sweet Elisabeth, but endearments weren't his thing. Even one like this, meant as provocation, undid her. For instead of sneering, his voice had sounded rough with something beyond anger, something that plucked at the taut threads of her control.

Before she had time to ponder what that was, or move out of reach, it was too late—he was holding her, his head swooping down to hers.

More to the point, she didn't *want* to move. What she wanted, with a yearning that belied all her stern self-talk, was to be right where she was.

His powerful arm wrapped around the bare flesh of her back and it felt like heaven as he pulled her to him. Heaven and hell together, for despite her excitement she knew she'd regret this when sanity returned.

Yet knowing and acting sensibly were two separate things.

His other hand gripped her skull and tilted it back as his mouth found hers.

There was no hesitation, no bumping of noses, no instant of shock and denial. Instead it felt like the inevitable culmination of every taut, breathless moment she'd endured since he'd prowled across the terrace to where she sat at the pool.

As if she'd been waiting for just this!

His kiss, his embrace felt right.

So right it would have terrified Bess if she'd been thinking straight. Instead she acted on primal, urgent instinct. The fingers of one hand splayed across his chest, picking up the quick, hard thrum of his heart. Her other hand slid around his neck, tunnelling through springy, thick hair to tug him closer.

That hard mouth softened. This wasn't a punishing kiss. It didn't feel like retribution or anger, but something she'd missed and yearned for since Paris.

Tenderness. Companionship. Mutual pleasure.

A shudder racked her body and for a moment she even thought it originated in Jack's tall frame.

He moved his mouth, sliding it along hers, slipping his tongue between her lips, and without thought she opened for him, her heartbeat swelling to a triumphant rhythm as he took what she offered.

Yet it wasn't really taking. This was mutual. The tangle of tongues, the slow exploration was a dance of give and take as if they relearned each other. It was as familiar as breathing but new too, rich with appreciation of what they'd missed.

They'd missed. Jack as well as her.

Maybe it was that knowledge that weakened her defences. If he'd demanded, she'd have resisted. Instead this felt like a compulsion neither could resist. A force stronger than either of them. The idea was intriguing and irresistible.

How could she have forgotten his taste, rich, complex and addictive? How could she have gone so long without it?

Bess tilted her head, tugging him closer as she demanded more, arching back under the weight of his eager response.

His body might be hard but his kiss was pure delight. Her skin tingled all over as if bursting to life after almost a year of dormancy. Her blood throbbed hard on its way through her body and between her legs was a telltale softening as if she readied for far more than a kiss.

That might have dismayed her except at that moment Jack pressed his lips to her cheek, trailing fire as he nipped at that incredibly sensitive place below her ear.

'Elisabeth,' he growled and she felt it against her overheated flesh as much as heard it.

Jack didn't sound like a savvy negotiator. He sounded like a desperate man.

Desperate for *her*.

It's just sex. Physical attraction. Not love.

But the sexual connection she'd shared with Jack was the closest Bess had ever come to perfection. The nearest thing to love she knew now her mother had gone.

And she'd been so very, very lonely.

It was one thing to cut her losses and leave a relationship that wasn't good for her. It was another to resist Jack when he hungered for her, when his caresses were ardent and needy and felt like an invitation to paradise.

If she'd been more strong-willed maybe she'd have pushed him away. But she was flawed and fallible, overwhelmed by the urgency of her feelings for this man. And by his desperation that proved they were equals in this.

Jack didn't do desperate. His specialty was coolheaded logic. Strategy not impulse. Planning not emotion.

Surely this was new? The notion stirred a flicker of hope as well as need.

'Jack. Kiss me again.'

He did. Ravenously. Thoroughly. Decadently. Their mouths fused, tongues mating in a hungry dance that ignited an explosion of heat in her pelvis.

Bess wriggled her hips closer, seeking relief. His arm slid down her back, a hand clamping on her buttocks and hauling her against his hard groin.

That felt like bliss. The promise of relief for her consuming hunger.

His other hand stroked her neck. There was a tug then her bodice dragged low and friction abraded her nipples.

Bess gasped, realising he'd undone the halterneck of her dress. Jack swallowed the sound, murmuring a hoarse paean of praise that went straight to her head as his hand covered her breast and for a moment she forgot to breathe.

She'd missed this, missed him. Despite everything she'd craved his touch so badly.

Slowly Jack lifted his head. In the darkness it should have been impossible to read his expression but his eyes glittered so brightly she was sure she saw both triumph and desperation there.

The only sound was their harsh breaths, drowning out the lap of the sea.

'*Now* do you believe I missed you?' Gently his fingers squeezed her breast and she groaned as incendiary heat burst through her, fire sizzling under her skin, igniting every erogenous nerve centre in her body.

Bess didn't have words because without waiting for an answer, Jack bent low, his mouth closing over her nipple in a caress that made her arch back hard, offering herself to him.

Jack was the man who'd taught her about desire. About sex and fulfilment. He'd never stinted, always bestowing pleasure and he delivered now, his ministrations sending her higher and higher on the path to desperation.

He changed his embrace, lifting her almost off the ground with the palm tree at her back and his solid body supporting her at the front. She tried to focus on whether she should stop this and send him away. But how could she when every touch, every caress, even the stroke of his warm breath on her bare skin felt like everything she'd ever wanted?

She lost the battle for control when she heard his voice, so low she almost didn't catch the words. 'I need you. I don't know how I went so long without you. There's been no-one since you, Elisabeth.'

He took her other nipple in his mouth and drew, slow and strong until her blood heated to flashpoint and she wondered if she might climax there and then.

'Jack!' She didn't know if she shouted or whispered his name but the depth of her longing was there, plain as day. As if her quaking, taut body wasn't proof enough.

Yet it was his revelation that truly undid her.

Jack had been celibate since she left!

It didn't occur to her to doubt it. Jack never lied. The idea of him waiting all this time, for *her*... It shouldn't make a difference but it did.

He pressed closer, pinioning her against the tree, one hand cupping her breast and the other sliding up the silk of her skirt, bunching it to caress her bare thigh.

She heard a gasping sigh. His or hers? He kissed her again, slow and deliberate like the progress of his hand up her leg, giving her time to stop him.

Bess thought about it. She really did. For at least a second. Somewhere in the back of her brain she knew there was a reason she shouldn't do this. But what reason could outweigh the euphoria of this, just one last time?

His hand stopped at the damp lace between her legs. The feel of his hand there... It took everything she had not to thrust forward into his touch.

He pulled back, just enough so they could drag in air. His forehead rested against hers. 'I should stop. I can't take you up against a tree, no matter how much I want to.'

Bess's heart leapt. His words notched her arousal impossibly higher. At this moment there was nothing she desired more than Jack filling that aching void within her. She imagined taking him inside her and for a moment the world around her blurred.

The hand between her legs moved away and her eyes snapped open as he lifted his head.

His expression looked stark in the chiaroscuro of black

shadow and silver moonlight. With regret and guilt? His voice was pure gravel as he said, 'We came here to talk. Not—'

'I don't want to talk now.'

He nodded, his mouth turning down as he straightened, allowing more distance between them. His chest rose mightily as if he too had difficulty catching his breath. 'I understand. Tomorrow morning—'

'Not tomorrow morning. Now!'

Bess grabbed his upper arms, feeling his bunching biceps through the fine fabric of his shirt, and leaned in close. Jack held her easily, a frown digging into his forehead as he surveyed her.

Because he wasn't accustomed to her making demands? Because she'd swung from not wanting to be near him to wanting *him* so fast?

But it hadn't been fast. That was the problem. Marriage to Jack Reilly was bad for her but that didn't cancel out the fact that sex with him made her feel wonderful, whole and powerful in a way she hadn't known for almost a year.

He didn't release her. If anything his hold tightened. 'Elisabeth, are you sure?'

That, more than anything else, tipped the balance.

Jack could have followed through and taken her as they both wanted in that moment of sheer erotic excitement. Instead he pulled back and offered her space. Even now when she'd made it clear she desired him, he did something he'd never done before. He hesitated.

Her husband never hesitated when it came to taking what he wanted. Unless it was a ploy to heighten the sensual tension between them. But that wasn't the case now. He was giving her time to reconsider, handing her back power instead of using it to his own advantage. Giving her time to regroup and possibly reject him.

Bess's eyes rounded.

Jack had changed.

She had no doubt he could still be ruthless. But in this moment he wasn't pressing his advantage. He wasn't charming her or persuading her or even seducing her, though the feel of his muscled body against hers was a promise of pleasure to come.

Something swooped high and hard in her chest. A sudden soaring, as if an unseen weight she'd carried lifted.

He was putting her first.

Jack had always been unselfish during sex, ensuring she climaxed, often several times, before he did. But this was more. This was deliberately ceding control of a situation where he had an advantage.

A thrill ran through her that had nothing to do with his body against hers, or the way her libido had suddenly reactivated. This thrill ran deeper and more potent. It shook her certainties about their relationship.

Could it be that this wasn't just sex for him?

'It's all right,' he said when she didn't respond. 'It's fine to change your mind.'

Despite the swollen shaft of his arousal pressing against her belly, proof of his need.

She'd expected anger if they met again. Annoyance at least. Instead she found consideration and a mutual carnal hunger that had grown rather than diminished.

It swept away her good intentions and left her with nothing to guide her but instinct.

Bess lifted her hand to his throat, pressing her palm against damp skin and the heavy throb of his pulse. It made him seem almost vulnerable too, no longer calling the shots.

'I haven't changed my mind. I want you, Jack.'

She couldn't lie about that. No matter what was wrong with their marriage there was no evading the fact that *this* at least was real and right. And if it were the last time she'd experience his lovemaking, all the more reason to enjoy the moment while she could. Perhaps it would be a way of letting go, saying goodbye to the physical side of their relationship before moving on.

She didn't consciously form the words but suddenly she wanted him to know. 'There's been no-one for me either since Paris.'

'Elisabeth.' Just that, but something about the deep timbre of his voice curled her toes and made her melt against him.

A second later he swung her up into his embrace, one arm around her back and the other under her legs, holding her high against his chest. Above her stars swirled in the inky sky as he turned back the way they'd come.

The movement brought a tickle of soft air across her bare breasts and she fumbled with her bodice, pulling it up to cover herself.

'Leave it,' he growled. 'The view's perfect as it is.'

It sure was. From here she had a view of his firm, determined jaw and the proud planes of his chiselled face.

She'd taken one look at him when they'd met at her father's party and felt something dip and sway inside her. She realised later it was her heart, knocked off balance by a man who, while not the most handsome she'd met, was by far the most charismatic and attractive.

Then they'd got talking and she'd discovered there was so much more to him than his looks. She'd been delighted when he'd pursued their acquaintance. Over the moon when he'd suggested marriage, even though it was a convenient one rather than a love match.

'You're very quiet,' he murmured as they rejoined the path to the villas.

Did he think she was having second thoughts?

She should be. But if there was one thing Jack had taught her it was that love wasn't to be confused with sex. He'd never loved her but he was spectacularly adept at sharing physical pleasure. And she wasn't in love with him anymore. She refused to be.

But sex… Why not accept that there was still a spark between them? Why not be the sophisticate she'd never been before and separate physical enjoyment from emotions?

Tomorrow he'd return to his frenetic schedule and she probably wouldn't see him again. Her lungs cramped on the thought but she ignored that.

Belatedly she realised they'd passed her bungalow. 'Where are we going?'

'My place is just along here at the end of the track.' His gaze caught hers and she read the glint in his eyes. 'There's an unopened box of condoms in the bedside cabinet.' He shrugged, the movement of those broad shoulders shifting her higher against his chest. His strength called to something primitive and wholly feminine within her. 'Maybe they provided some in your villa too but I don't want to start something there that we can't finish.'

Bess hadn't thought about protection. She'd stopped taking the pill after she left Paris so she should have been more conscious of that.

But instead of berating herself, she was too busy replaying his words about not starting something he couldn't finish. Jack sounded as strung out as she and she couldn't help her fillip of delight.

Tonight *was* different between them.

In the past he'd set the pace in their lovemaking, though he'd always been careful to ensure she was eager for what they shared.

Initially that had been because she was inexperienced and later… Was it out of habit? Because their marriage had been devised by him to suit his needs? Or because she'd been so in love and so caught up in delight at how special he made her feel in bed that it had never occurred to her to take the lead in intimacy?

Tonight she'd taken the lead, insisting this was what she wanted when he would have pulled away.

She curled her hand around the back of his neck, gently scoring his flesh with her nails.

Bess felt his shudder and his misstep and a smile curved her mouth. She enjoyed the sense of power.

Jack's stride lengthened and it seemed only seconds before they reached his accommodation. But instead of putting her down he somehow managed to keep her in his arms and unlock the door, nudging it shut behind them as he strode through the vast living space to the bedroom.

Then they were on the bed, his weight pressing her into the mattress and a great ache started up inside her at the delicious familiarity of it. At the thousands of memories that rose. Of the ecstasy they'd shared, the optimistic hopes she'd dreamt in Jack's arms.

She swallowed hard. Her dreams of romance had shattered. She'd never go down the track again, not with this man. For she was determined to conquer that hopeless yearning.

Instead she'd take tonight for what it was. Fleeting physical pleasure. Jack was good at that and she might as well make the most of it.

'Elisabeth? Where have you gone?'

Even in the darkness, reaching across to the bedside cabinet and its store of condoms, he'd noticed the change in her.

Jack was far too prescient. She preferred it when he was too busy reacting to sexual stimuli to read her thoughts.

She reached up, grabbed both sides of his open collar and pulled hard. A button hit her chin as his shirt ripped open, then her palms were on his chest, soaking up his heat, feeling the friction from that dusting of dark hair across his pectoral muscles.

He made an inarticulate sound at the back of his throat then galvanised into movement, undoing his trousers and tearing open a condom packet with his teeth.

His urgency spurred her on, pushing his shirt off his shoulders. They became entangled and he rose from the bed, shrugging out of his shirt and shoving the rest of his clothes down in one urgent movement.

There was enough light through the open curtains for her to appreciate the spectacular view as he toed off his shoes and freed himself of his clothes.

Jack had a magnetism that was accentuated by his bespoke clothes. In public he was urbane, rarely allowing his ruthlessness to show through. But naked he stripped down to a figure so purely, elementally masculine that Bess suppressed a sigh. With his wide, straight shoulders, narrow hips and powerfully muscled chest and thighs he might have modelled as a warrior for some ancient sculptor.

'How fond are you of that dress?' he asked as he rolled on protection.

'It's new and I like it.'

'Then take it off unless you want it damaged like my shirt.'

Bess blinked. Never, no matter how urgent their need, had Jack threatened to tear her clothes off.

She liked it. Liked it too much.

But what was too much? Tonight was about giving in to simple lust.

She almost didn't move. What would it be like to have those large hands tearing the silk from her body? He'd do it, too. She read determination in the set of his jaw and the twitch of his fingers as he stepped towards the bed.

But these days she lived on a limited budget, her work not particularly well paid, so her new dresses were real luxuries. Or maybe she wasn't as bold as she thought. Either way she found herself unzipping the red silk and shimmying out of it, tossing it aside as Jack knelt at the end of the bed. Her heart beat a crazy tattoo as if trying to leap out of her chest.

'Better,' he murmured, reaching for her lace knickers. 'But these have to go.'

Bess arched up so he could pull them down. Instead, hooking his fingers in the top, he simply yanked and the delicate fabric tore free. Eyes wide, she watched him toss the pale lace over his shoulder.

Excitement shivered through her and that pulse between her thighs became an urgent throb.

'You like that, do you?' His smile was a caress, the rumbling note of his voice pure seduction. 'I hadn't realised till now that my wife had a taste for such things.'

She would have protested his choice of words—*my wife* when she was in all but legality his ex—but her throat had dried with excitement. For he was prowling up the bed on all fours, a sensual predator, and she'd never felt more aroused in her life.

One large hand covered her thigh and pushed it wide, then her other thigh, leaving her wide open. His smile died and she heard as well as saw him heft a deep breath as he surveyed her.

Bess gloried in the power of her feminine allure as she watched Jack battle for control. He was breathing hard, the tendons in his neck standing proud and his arousal impressive. She reached for him but he shook his head and moved to lower himself between her legs, his breath hot against her pubic hair.

'No!'

His head jerked up. 'No?'

She felt his tension, his body strained and hard. She shook her head. 'No time for that.' Though she adored it when he caressed her there. 'I need you *with* me.'

He moved before she'd finished speaking, rising up her body so this time when he lowered himself they were torso to torso, pelvis to pelvis, setting off a shower of sparks where they touched.

'You're not going to stop me doing this too, are you?' He didn't wait for a response, cupping her breast with one hand and kissing the other.

Bess arched high, clasping his head to her breast, setting her teeth against the scream of pleasure forming on her tongue.

She remembered intimacy with him being mind-numbingly

good but this… Every atom in her body was attuned to his touch, her muscles clenching in eager readiness for his possession. As if her body had been dormant before this, waiting for his caress to bring her back to life.

The thought terrified her but before she could dwell on it he lifted his head, eyes holding hers as he shifted higher, settling between her hips and aligning their bodies.

Bess sighed with relief as he moved, watching her as he slid slow and deep, until they were no longer two separate beings but one. The wonder of it made her heartbeat stumble as if it were the first time all over again. As if all the world hung on this moment.

Jack's shoulders rose and fell, his chest deliciously hard against hers. His breath was a hot caress on her face. His eyes were unreadable in this light but his regard was so intense instinct warned that maybe sex wasn't as simple as she'd thought.

But before she could think that through, Jack moved and she responded, the thrust of his possession calling to all that was female and eager inside her. She lifted her knees, wrapped her arms around him and matched her movements to his.

Still those dark, glittering eyes held hers as if they saw deep into her soul, to the needy woman she hadn't yet managed to eradicate fully.

'Elisabeth.' Their tempo picked up and she caught her breath. He lowered his head, his lips brushing hers. 'Come for me.'

His hand was at her breast, his thumb hard on her nipple as he trailed his mouth across her cheek then captured her earlobe with his teeth.

That was all it took. His words in her ears, the lightning bolt of erotic energy from there to her nipple to her pelvis. His thrusts turned urgent and she heard a high-pitched keening as he drove deep. Her taut body reached its limit and spasmed in ecstasy. A second later he followed, spending himself in frantic shudders that reignited her own rapture, his deep-throated groan of completion primal and somehow moving.

Bess held him tight in the glowing aftermath, her body and mind reluctant to return to earth. When she did it was to notice how tightly he wrapped her to him, rolling onto his back so she lay boneless above him.

Her eyes drifted shut as she promised herself just a moment or two in his arms before moving away.

Her last, confusing thought was that she hadn't expected simple lust to be like this. Her imagination was working overtime because, as peace settled over her, this felt like more than mere physical satisfaction.

It felt like Jack had filled the emotional emptiness she'd experienced ever since that day of awful revelation in Paris. If sleep hadn't claimed her, she'd have been appalled.

CHAPTER FOUR

'DEAR FRIENDS, WE ARE gathered here to celebrate the loving union of Freya and Michael.'

Jack watched the bride and groom turn to each other. They looked radiant, as if they couldn't believe life could be so good.

Had he ever looked that way?

Of course not. Since childhood he'd never believed the romantic fiction of soul mates. His parents had ensured that.

Yet he'd been happy on his wedding day. Exultant even, knowing Elisabeth was the perfect partner to help him achieve his goals.

But she'd been more. There'd been no denying the instant attraction between them that had only grown as they became better acquainted. She wasn't just beautiful, well-connected and with the social graces he required. Despite her inexperience, the sexual chemistry between them had been off the charts.

His attention shifted to her, standing to one side of her cousin. His wife was stunning. Just looking at her shortened his breath and stirred his blood.

She wore a slim-fitting dress of burnished dark orange. It made her glow like some fabled treasure or a bright flame. That was a better analogy. He thought of how she'd gone up in flames last night, of how their urgent passion had seared him. He'd known they'd still be spectacular together but he hadn't been prepared for the conflagration that had engulfed him.

Had ten months without sex heightened his senses to acute levels? Or the piquant mix of unresolved emotions?

He'd kissed her and she'd all but destroyed him. He'd been on the verge of taking her against a tree on the edge of the beach where anyone could have found them. That would have been a fatal error. It had required every scintilla of self-control to pull back as if he'd had second thoughts about sex.

As if!

But better that Elisabeth be the one to insist so vehemently that she wanted him than for him to seduce her. That would have been disastrous. Jack refused to allow her any excuse to withdraw from him again. That simply wasn't an option.

Besides, it had been invigorating having his wife make sexual demands. She'd never been coy or passive, but nor had she ever dictated the direction of their sexual encounters.

She'd changed. And despite the indignation, anger and even hurt he still felt over her dumping him, he couldn't help but enjoy the feisty woman he'd encountered last night. He looked forward to being with her again.

He looked at her profile, her approving smile as she watched the bride and groom. As if sensing his stare she shifted her weight and half turned to look over her shoulder before turning back to the couple.

Satisfaction bloomed deep in Jack's belly. She might be trying to hide it but Elisabeth was as aware of him as he was of her.

He'd been annoyed that she'd slipped out of his bed after he'd fallen asleep around dawn. But it was just as well. He'd lost count of the number of times they'd had each other through the night but he suspected that if he'd woken with her in his arms this morning he wouldn't have been able to resist taking her again. They'd have been late for the ceremony.

His mouth curved into a tight smile.

He needed to allow her some space, or at least the illusion

of it. *She* needed to come to *him*. And after last night he had no doubt that was exactly what she'd do.

'You may now kiss the bride.'

Jack looked at the embracing couple and back to Elisabeth. She was grinning with delight, her eyes sparkling.

He'd never wanted her more.

He had a flash of memory, of looking down at her the day they'd married. She'd suggested a small wedding. He'd insisted on a big event. Space for several hundred guests. An elaborate reception. His staff had booked up exclusive accommodation for the international VIPs and they'd had to negotiate the release of approved wedding photos in order to avoid helicopters and drones invading their privacy. Even her dress had been altered to include an impressive, long train which would look perfect in the larger venue. Because their wedding was part of his plans to extend his commercial interests. Cultivating key European policy makers and investors had been vital.

It hadn't been the wedding his bride would have chosen. But when he'd turned at the end of the ceremony to kiss her, she'd looked up at him with stars in her eyes and a smile that stole his breath as effectively as a punch to the solar plexus.

She'd been happy then. He was sure of it. And she'd trusted him.

What they'd had was good, far better than he'd anticipated, and he intended to get that, and her, back.

The bridal couple turned and he moved forward to congratulate them. He mightn't buy into the idea of romantic love but he sincerely hoped his friend would be happy with his new bride.

As he intended to be with his wayward wife.

'You're going to be so happy,' Bess said, hugging her cousin, 'I just know it.'

Michael held Freya's hand tight as if he couldn't bear not to be touching her and Bess felt her chest contract. Because they were so ecstatic, as they should be. They were so well-matched.

And because she was just a little jealous of the joy they'd found?

No. Not jealous. She didn't begrudge them anything. Even if this intimate beachside celebration was the sort of wedding she'd have chosen for herself if she'd had the option.

She just wished… No, no point in wishing for the impossible.

'Thanks Bess. It was wonderful you could attend.' Freya kissed her cheek and dropped her voice. 'I know it must be hard, celebrating a wedding when your marriage—'

'It was absolutely my pleasure. You know I wouldn't have missed it for the world.'

A deep voice came from just behind her, evoking a lush curl of decadent heat low in her body. 'Nor would I,' Jack said. 'I'm glad you finally put him out of his misery and agreed to marry him, Freya. It's hard doing business with a man who can't concentrate.'

There was laughter all round and then it was time for goodbyes.

Bess hugged Michael, suddenly emotional. 'You look after my cousin, won't you?'

He nodded, serious eyes belying that easy smile. 'You know I will. I love her.'

Something rolled over inside her. Joy, she told herself, even as she had to force herself not to watch as Jack embraced Freya. This wasn't about her and Jack, or the fact that the love in their marriage had been all on one side. She should have known it was a recipe for heartbreak.

Instead she grinned at Michael then stepped back so the other guests could say their farewells.

Somehow she found herself standing next to Jack and those unsettled emotions ramped even higher.

She'd spent the whole morning *not* catching his eye. Not

because she was ashamed of last night but because she knew it changed nothing between them. Like the other wedding guests he'd be flying out today. They'd all arrived a few days ago and already had their holiday whereas she'd been unable to get here until the day before the ceremony.

The point was she and Jack had had breakup sex and now they'd return to their separate lives. She could only hope their night of scorching passion had burned away some of her unresolved feelings for him. Like cauterising an open wound.

She lifted her chin higher and focused on smiling. For she *was* happy for Freya. Even if her own dreams were in tatters.

Catching the direction of her thoughts her mouth pursed. Those were old dreams. She had new ones now. A fulfilling career that would take her to interesting places and satisfy her desire to do some good in the world. As for personal relationships, there was plenty of time for those in the future.

They watched as the bridal couple boarded the tender that would take them to the extravagantly beautiful yacht for their honeymoon.

Just as it should be, a honeymoon spent alone together, not traipsing to one society event after another, more concerned with business than building a real relationship.

She'd made the right decision, walking out on Jack. They were just too different, with completely different needs.

Ten minutes later they'd waved goodbye to the newlyweds and the other guests had said their farewells, heading off to their villas to collect their luggage before leaving.

Yet Jack lingered. Surely he didn't want a post-mortem of what had happened last night?

They hadn't been alone since she'd left his bed and that suited her perfectly. What they'd shared last night had stunned her, even knowing his virility and how physically compatible they were. It felt as if she'd tapped into something elemental, something far stronger than simple physical desire or the culmination of her confused feelings. She didn't want to analyse too closely for she feared if she did she'd discover she was still too weak where he was concerned. Far simpler to view it as cathartic sex as they shed their last links.

Bess gave one last wave in the direction of the yacht and turned to him, not meeting his eyes.

'I suppose this is goodbye, Jack. The flight's leaving soon.' She stopped, swallowing a sudden constriction in her throat. Stupid to feel emotional. She wasn't foolish enough to believe last night had meant anything but a release of built-up sexual tension. 'We didn't get to discuss the divorce papers. Can I assume you're ready to sign them now?'

His straight eyebrows arrowed down in the middle of his forehead. 'You're not leaving?'

Bess shook her head. 'Not me, I'm staying for a week. But I know you'll be eager to return to work.'

'Not necessarily.'

He paused and she did what she'd vowed not to, met those stunning blue eyes. As usual they didn't reveal much. But there was something, something that made heat trickle from her tight chest down to her pelvis. Her breasts rose on a quick breath as she remembered last night. His urgency, his tenderness, the way it seemed he couldn't get enough of her, no matter how sated they were.

She'd felt the same. As if she were frantically hoarding up memories to take with her when they separated today.

Bess snapped her head around to stare at the huge yacht, already leaving the island behind.

'I thought I might stay on. *If you are.*'

Her eyes rounded as she digested his words. He wanted to spend more time with her? He'd even delay his return to work?

'You'd change your plans to stay longer because of me?'

Swift as thought, some emotion rippled across his features but she couldn't define it. Discomfort? She knew Jack prided himself on his forward planning and his commitment to work.

Did he think it weakness to consider altering his schedule on the spur of the moment to be with her?

Bess reeled at the possibilities. It had never occurred to her that Jack might want more than one night. She'd told herself she'd only wanted sex to stop the clamouring in her blood and to get him out of her system.

She'd lied to herself.

Excitement bubbled in her veins and she tried to ignore it, for this was important and she needed to think straight.

'It's not over between us, Elisabeth. Can't you feel it? I'm not ready to let you walk away and after last night I don't think you're ready to go.'

Bess couldn't believe what she was hearing. He didn't think their marriage over? She opened her mouth to speak but what he said next stole the words from her tongue.

'Work can wait. You're staying a week. Why don't I stay too?' His eyes held hers and she felt herself sinking into that deep blue as if she dived into her own private ocean.

Work could wait?

The ground trembled beneath her feet as if from a continent-splitting earthquake.

Never had she expected to hear such a thing from Jack Reilly. Work was his number one priority, his *only* priority, and always had been.

'We could talk.'

Bess stared, instinctively shuffling her feet wider. Because another tremor tilted the ground beneath her soles.

He wanted to *talk*?

It was unheard of.

She'd always enjoyed chatting with Jack. He was clever, interesting and he listened. But they never discussed their marriage. Jack had decided what he wanted, set the parameters on the day he proposed and made clear since that those parameters weren't up for negotiation.

Bess felt her jaw sag in amazement then snapped her mouth closed.

'We can stay in separate villas if you prefer. I'm sure they can accommodate me.'

She blinked. He really was going to change his plans? Put off his business commitments, to spend time with her?

She knew how much work went into organising his schedule. How every hour and half hour were allocated with precision. In all the time she'd known him he'd never put anything ahead of his business goals.

Now he wanted to do that for her.

As if she were more important than the valuable negotiations he no doubt had in hand. More important than the business opportunities he'd miss to be with her.

He'd never put her first before.

A warm, fuzzy feeling bloomed and she wanted to hug it close. It felt precious. An unexpected gift. Her husband had always been generous but their marriage, and therefore she, had always come second to business.

When she'd first seen Jack yesterday she'd expected anger. Her departure must have bruised his pride as well as being inconvenient for his plans. He was a man accustomed to getting his way.

Yet here he was saying their marriage wasn't over, wanting to talk.

Despite Bess's caution, her heart swelled with precarious hope. Was there a chance to mend what was broken between them? Perhaps he *did* care for her but hadn't been good at expressing that?

She stared into that bold, handsome face and wondered if it could be true. Or was this some devious ploy to make her pay for disrupting his convenient marriage?

But Jack had never been devious with her. In fact his propensity to be up-front about everything, while laudable in theory, had been difficult to bear sometimes.

Would you rather he'd pretended to love you?
'Elisabeth?'

Was it wishful thinking or did she really hear the tiniest echo of vulnerability in his question?

No, that was taking things too far. But here he was, in good faith suggesting they spend time together and talk. How could she say no? If there was the tiniest possibility they could salvage their marriage and turn it into something real, she had to take it.

She cleared her throat. 'I think that's a great idea.'

They started with dinner on the private terrace of his bungalow. The food was excellent and Jack couldn't have ordered a more spectacular sunset. Elisabeth sighed appreciatively, exclaiming over the sky turning pink, orange and gold, its colours reflected in the sea.

But it was Elisabeth who was gorgeous. Jack couldn't take his eyes off her.

Their attraction had always been strong but now it felt like a compulsion. Was it just because of those months apart? Listening to her sigh jolted him back to last night and her throaty cries as he pleasured her.

Heat crawled up his neck and around his hairline as he fought not to think about how close and convenient his bed was.

Instead he made himself concentrate on small talk. He needed to get her to relax and win her trust. He hadn't missed her wariness when he'd suggested staying on here. More than wariness, she'd looked completely stunned.

Did she really think he'd give up their marriage so easily? She didn't know him at all in that case.

'Where are you living now?' she asked as she reached for more seafood.

'Still in Paris, in the same hotel.'

Elisabeth paused, her hands on the serving spoons. 'In

Paris? I thought you'd have moved on by now. Weren't you thinking of Germany or the Middle East next?'

He shrugged and took a sip of crisp white wine. It was a fine vintage but he wasn't doing it justice because his mind was focused on his wife. It would be too easy to say something that would reopen the chasm between them when that was the last thing he wanted.

'It's not so far from Paris to Berlin or any of the other major German cities. Besides, there's been plenty to keep me busy in France.'

He refused to admit to Elisabeth, barely even acknowledged it himself, that he hadn't *wanted* to leave Paris. There was no logical explanation. Just a gut-deep reluctance connected to the memory of her ditching him there. The need to have her walk back in through the very same door she'd closed so quietly behind her and resume their life together.

A psychologist would say something about his childhood scars and his parents' abandonment. But Jack knew he'd got over that long ago. This was solely about his wife and getting her back.

Yet he couldn't bring himself to tackle a new city without her beside him. It had nothing to do with business. He could succeed without her, now he'd developed more contacts in Europe. The success of his projects spoke for themselves. Instead some deep-seated instinct told him he couldn't merely shrug off her desertion and move on.

Elisabeth would come back to him. She'd walk into that Paris suite again, into his bed and into his life and *then* he'd be ready for his next move.

'It's an attractive city, don't you think?'

She transferred some food onto her plate and put down the serving spoons. 'I suppose so.'

One eyebrow rose. 'I thought you enjoyed the restaurants and galleries. And everyone raves about the shopping.'

'I'm not much of a shopper.'

It was true. Elisabeth always looked just as she should, the perfect outfit for each occasion, well-groomed and sophisticated. She'd spent his money on expensive gowns for expensive occasions but retail therapy wasn't her thing. That set her apart from most of the women he'd known.

'But you enjoyed the exhibitions I took you to.' They'd attended several exclusive black tie gallery events as well as the usual charity galas, performances and dinners.

She swallowed a mouthful of food then nodded. 'Yes, I enjoyed those.' She lifted one shoulder. 'But you can't spend every day filling in time at galleries and restaurants.'

Jack frowned. That was exactly what partners of his business associates did. Ladies who lunched and shopped and had spa days.

'You were lonely?' That hadn't occurred to him. She'd always seemed content, right up until the day she announced she was leaving. 'You'd have made friends there in time.'

She put down her cutlery with a clatter. 'What would be the point? Your schedule meant we wouldn't put down roots because we'd move again in a couple of months.'

His eyes narrowed. More than once she'd mentioned buying a place within commuting distance of the city. He hadn't been against the idea, but it didn't fit into his five-year plan. Perhaps sometime in the future.

'Anyway, I did have some friends there.'

Her look was pure challenge and she sat straighter. He knew they were on dangerous ground.

'You mean Lara Cartwright.'

She nodded. 'Marriage didn't give you the right to dictate who I could be friends with.'

His heart sank. He remembered only snippets of that night. The migraine that had been the first sign of the flu that had felled him. He'd spend the evening in throbbing pain and sensitive to light. The last thing he'd felt like had been going to a gala and giving a speech. Then he'd been confronted with the paparazzi's stories about his wife, just when he was in the middle of tricky negotiations with a blue-blooded CEO who already considered Jack a brash colonial. Normally he'd let his work speak for itself but that deal was the key to unlocking several he had his eye on.

'I wasn't dictating, I was advising. And she wasn't a close friend, was she?'

As soon as he spoke he knew he'd said the wrong thing.

Elisabeth's chin came up. 'We were at school together and she needed a friend in Paris.'

'She might have needed a friend but she had no right to drag you into the gutter press.' The woman seemed to delight in flaunting her reputation for scandal.

The details of that evening were blurry but he remembered the photos of the two women leaving an exclusive Parisian bar. They were arm in arm, heads together as if sharing secrets, Lara waving a half-empty martini glass and the angle of the photo making it look like they were unsteady on their feet. The caption had implied they'd been carousing all afternoon and speculated maliciously about Elisabeth having more in common with her friend than the public realised.

'Lara didn't drag me anywhere. She can't help what the press writes.'

Jack drew a slow breath, knowing he had to back down. 'You're right. It wasn't her fault.' He twisted the stem of his wineglass, watching the pale liquid swirl. 'I know how the press twist and sensationalise things. I overreacted. I'm sorry.'

Elisabeth stared as if seeing him for the first time.

She blinked and those remarkable amber eyes darkened as her pupils dilated. Her lips parted and his breath hitched as arousal hit him like a hammer blow. It was instant and complete, blood surging low in his body, impairing his train of thought. He wanted to lean across the table and kiss her. Haul her onto his lap and set her astride his burgeoning erection.

He wanted…

* * *

He was sorry?

Bess wanted to believe it so badly it scared her. His high-handed attitude that night had cut her to the heart. Because it reinforced that she wasn't a wife to him but an asset to be used as he saw fit.

He'd been furious about the press reports. When they returned from the charity gala he'd stalked off to his study while she dithered, trying to decide whether to pack and leave. Then she'd heard a thud and found Jack sprawled on the floor, delirious. His temperature had spiked alarmingly as the flu hit him hard and fast. By the time he was recuperating she'd made up her mind to go. It had been easier not to linger to rehash what clearly couldn't be fixed.

Or could it? Had it been a mistake to leave him?

At the time it had seemed her only option. Jack's attitude had been so unyielding.

Bess shot to her feet, turning towards the sea, arms wrapped around herself. She didn't know what to think.

'Elisabeth.'

He was right behind her. She felt his breath on her hair and despite everything her shiver wasn't one of distaste. She shouldn't have gone to bed with him last night. It made her less protected against him.

When he spoke again it was in that deep, gravel-over-velvet voice that made her weak. 'I don't remember what I said that night because I was already feeling sick. But believe me I regret it.'

Another pause. 'I do remember the press reports and worrying that it was the excuse the Count needed to convince his board not to do business with an upstart Australian. I knew he favoured someone from his own set.' Bess heard a sigh. 'But it was crass of me to ask you to give up your friend.'

Slowly she turned. They were so close she read every nuance of his expression and for once he held nothing back.

She saw contrition, regret, and an intensity that ran like fire through her blood. Her heart rolled over in her chest.

Jack's apology didn't solve the problem at the root of their marriage. But it was significant. He hadn't been at his best that night so he hadn't been thinking clearly. His sincerity now showed him willing to change.

Change enough to make their marriage real? To *care* for her as she cared for him?

She couldn't jump to conclusions. But it was a positive sign, and she clung to that.

'Apology accepted.' His smile unfurled and she felt her heart lift with it. 'Thank you.'

He gently brushed her hair off her cheek, igniting a trail of sparks from his touch.

Her heart hammered with excitement and trepidation as he cupped her face in his big hands. Was she making the biggest mistake of her life agreeing to this week together?

Or was there truly a chance to turn their marriage into something real?

CHAPTER FIVE

'I'M GOING TO pay you back for this, Jack Reilly!'

Jack lifted his eyes, taking in the sumptuous sight of his naked wife spreadeagled on the bed before him. Despite the tension of extreme arousal, his mouth kicked up in a grin.

She was his, all his.

'I look forward to it.'

He paused, his gaze lingering on the cloth belt from her silky bathrobe that he'd used to tie her wrists to the headboard. It wasn't a tight knot and if she'd really wanted she could have freed herself. But she'd been too busy sighing and writhing in ecstasy to realise that.

With pillows propped behind her and her arms up above her head, her body arched high, her breasts standing proud and alluring. But for the moment he'd moved on from there.

Still holding her eyes, he lowered his mouth to the silky skin of her inner thigh and felt her legs tremble and tighten around him.

'I mean it.' Her jaw jutted. 'Only I won't use a cloth to tie you up. I'll get handcuffs.'

Blood shot to his already engorged penis and he had to close his eyes. The sight of her spread before him was too much temptation for a man who'd gone without for ten whole months. A mere week together had been nowhere near enough to take the edge off his hunger for her.

But with eyes shut his imagination was free to conjure images of Elisabeth trying to turn the tables on him. He'd never had a penchant for handcuffs, but with his wife anything was possible.

Like the fact that each day, each hour, sex with her was better than before.

'Is that supposed to scare me?' He licked up her leg and across to the knot of nerve endings where she was most sensitive, and was rewarded with a moan of pleasure as her thighs turned lax and opened around him. He breathed in the dusky rose scent of her arousal. 'You can tie me up as much as you like, Elisabeth. I won't try to stop you.'

He enjoyed those times when she took the initiative. She was a generous, passionate woman. She'd never left him unsatisfied. But even if she had, Jack took almost more pleasure from watching her climax than he did from his own orgasms.

He burrowed his head between her thighs and focused again on bringing her to the edge.

It didn't take much. She was already primed.

'Jack Reilly! Stop that now!'

He jerked his head up.

Her face was flushed, eyes glittering brighter than polished gems. She didn't look angry so much as on edge. 'I *told* you.' She pouted. 'I need *you*.'

Jack told himself it was sexual arousal speaking. But her words lodged deep within him.

She needed him.

Enough to stay with him this time?

His heart bumped hard against his ribs. He'd experienced his fair share of desertion, starting with his parents. It was his least favourite thing.

He'd told himself as he secured her wrists to the bed head that this was just a sex game. He'd wanted Elisabeth mindless with pleasure. But even so he couldn't miss the significance of her bound hands.

He was a modern man. He'd never forcibly restrain her

from leaving him. Yet there was something deeply satisfying about having her exactly where he wanted her. Solace for the gut-rending memory of her walking out on him.

'Please, Jack.' She blinked and he saw her eyelashes spike as tears welled.

Instantly he moved to kneel astride her as he reached for the cloth that bound her. He tossed the sash aside and lifted her hands to his mouth, kissing the inside of her wrists and her palms. 'I didn't mean to scare you.'

'Scare me?' Her fingers curled strongly around his. 'You didn't scare me, you frustrated me.' He looked down and met eyes glowing gemstone-bright with emotion. 'I love... I like that you're so unselfish, giving me all those climaxes, but I want to *hold* you.' She paused, drawing a deep breath that made her raspberry-tipped breasts wobble invitingly. 'I want to be with you this time.'

Jack's lungs expanded as he fought not to read too much into her words. After all, this was what he'd wanted, Elisabeth so deeply in thrall to him sexually that there'd be no more talk of separate lives.

This week had gone exactly as he'd hoped. More so. Perhaps he should have made time for a honeymoon after all.

He couldn't remember a better time. Not even the highs of his first business successes or the satisfaction of bringing much-needed assistance to people in remote areas who rarely received benefits like free power.

A soft hand skimmed down his body, past his thundering chest, over abdominal muscles that twitched at her light touch, to encircle his erection.

Jack swallowed hard, his mouth drying.

This was why he'd tied her up—her ability to stop him thinking. To make him even more crazy for her so he couldn't concentrate on seducing her.

Her hand slid up his length, squeezing with just the right pressure. Amazing to think she hadn't been with a man before him. No other woman had ever aroused him so easily and so totally.

'Jack?'

He shook his head, trying to clear his thoughts as he took her wrist and pulled her hand away, ignoring an inner howl of protest.

'Together then,' he grunted.

It was what he wanted more than anything, to be locked with Elisabeth. Yet as he watched her lips curve in a cat-with-the-cream smile, something shuddered through him.

A warning?

A worry that instead of turning his wife into putty in his hands, that's exactly what she'd done to him.

These feelings rising within him, the ever-present yearning ache to be with her, gave him pause.

He didn't do vulnerable. Not since he was a kid, at the mercy of his unreliable parents. But that's how he felt now, as if Elisabeth had scraped his emotions raw. As if, despite him having the upper hand, she'd unwittingly discovered a vulnerability in him that even he hadn't recognised.

She lifted her arms to him and he'd never seen anyone more beautiful or enticing. It was hard, almost impossible to resist. But these unfamiliar emotions unsettled him. Who knew what Elisabeth would see in his eyes when he was at his most unguarded?

So instead of sinking into her embrace, he sat back a little. 'Roll over, Elisabeth. Onto your hands and knees.'

His voice was gruff, not with command but anticipation. Anticipation he saw reflected in her bright eyes, for his wife always enjoyed sex that way.

Even so she hesitated, her lips forming a delicious pout, as if he'd denied her something she was looking forward to. She opened her mouth as if to speak but he forestalled her, bending to nip her earlobe and tell her in words of one syllable exactly what he wanted to do with her, while his hand toyed between her legs.

She sighed and trembled and, grabbing his face between her palms, kissed him hard and long as if she couldn't contain her rising hunger either.

He was just deciding it didn't matter what position they used, as long as he was inside her, when she pulled back and, with a long, scorching look, rolled over.

She was all sinuous lines and smooth curves and the sight of her rising on her hands and knees before him drained the blood from his brain. She was barely on all fours when his hands were on her, curving around her hips, splaying across taut buttocks and smoothing up to her narrow waist. Jack leaned closer, his erection hard between her cheeks as he cupped her breasts. A low sound escaped his throat. Something primal and possessive, grounded in excitement so profound it felt bigger than him, bigger than them.

'Bess!'

There was a world of craving in his voice and in his body as he notched himself against her. His hands were damp as he stroked her then gently pinched her nipples.

She gasped and the tremor that ran through her passed through him too.

He wanted to take his time and enjoy the sight of her, so slender yet so strong and feminine, so perfect. But his senses betrayed him. The feel of her breasts in his hands, and her bottom pressing back against him. The scent of wild rose and eager woman that lodged at the back of his nostrils, surely the most effective pheromone on the planet. The sound of her broken breathing.

Jack bent over her, grazing his teeth over the side of her neck, rewarded by her jolt of arousal before kissing her there and drawing in the unique taste of her.

It was too much. He straightened, taking himself in hand to guide his way to that sweetest spot between her legs.

There. Just…there.

He slid forward into welcoming heat then paused, gently pushing between her shoulder blades so she changed the angle of her body and he slid home, right to the heart of her.

'Okay?'

His voice was so rough it should have been incomprehensible, yet he heard her whisper, 'Perfect.'

That was all it took to slice through his last effort at restraint.

This was too good. Bess was too exquisite. Grabbing her hips, he withdrew then pushed home again and felt sparks prickle his senses. She circled her hips and that came close to blowing the back off his skull.

Jack slipped his hand around her, palming her abdomen and straight down to her moist core. This time when he withdrew and drove home he stroked her as she pushed back against him.

Another withdrawal, another thrust and then he crashed apart, his life force pulsing hard into Bess's exquisite heat. He felt the spasms of her orgasm, heard her cry of ecstasy as she arched back towards him.

Jack wrapped his arm around her, planting his other hand on the bed as he leaned down to cover her, skin to skin, his crashing heart to her back, his urgent breaths against her fragrant neck.

He felt like together they'd climbed the stars and ridden a blazing comet.

Even the shared aftershocks were bliss and totally overwhelming.

He'd given up thinking. Given up planning.

There was just this, the pair of them together.

Perfect.

'Come back to Paris with me.'

Bess's breathing faltered as the words penetrated her haze of well-being.

She opened her eyes to find Jack lying on his side, watching her. His gaze was bright and in the early morning light she could swear she saw something new there. Something that hadn't been there when they'd lived together.

Silently she stared back, trying to catalogue his expression. Tenderness definitely, like the light stroke of his fingers on her bare waist and hip. But something more. Something more...profound.

Need?

That was the word that sprang into her dazzled mind.

Was it possible Jack *needed* her? Not for his business plans, but for something more personal?

Her heart fluttered.

His success in the past year proved that whatever he'd once thought, he was capable of achieving his business goals without her at his side.

'Elisabeth, you're not saying anything.'

She blinked. Last night as they made love he'd called her Bess, and something tight and hard inside her had loosened and fallen away. He'd done it when they were as close as a man and a woman could be. It had made her feel that maybe things had changed and they shared something more than sex. That they were building a different sort of connection.

Jack had always preferred her full name. She suspected he enjoyed its formality, the reminder that her family, while impoverished, was aristocratic. After all, he'd chosen her as his bride for her privileged connections.

She stared into his eyes and found them unreadable. Whatever she'd thought she saw a moment ago had gone.

She spoke carefully. 'I'm just surprised.'

'Why?'

His hand tightened at her hip before resuming its slow, soothing slide. She felt her body respond. She wanted to arch into his touch as nerve endings tickled and the beginnings of sexual arousal stirred in her sated body.

All week it had been the same. Jack only had to touch her, or sometimes just look at her with that heavy-lidded expression, and she was ready for him again.

That scared her on the few occasions she'd thought about where this week was heading. Most times she'd been too craven to think about it, preferring to tell herself it was a week out of time. For despite what they'd agreed, they'd done little talking. When they did, it was about inconsequential things. As if neither wanted to shatter the magic they shared.

She'd been a coward, afraid that when they did discuss their relationship it would end forever.

She covered his hand with hers and moved it to the mattress between them. She couldn't think when he caressed her and this was too important for distraction.

'We only agreed to a week together.'

Already he was shaking his head. 'You really think a week is enough?' He paused, eyes narrowing as he dropped his gaze to her mouth then lower and she saw heat spark in those cobalt depths.

One thing that hadn't changed was their sexual connection. If anything it had grown stronger here on the island. She'd told herself it was because of the time they'd spent apart. But a fear was growing that recent abstinence had little to do with it and Jack had tapped into a need for him that she just couldn't eradicate.

'What do you want, Jack?'

'You.' The answer came instantly and despite her reservations elation rose. She felt it as a welling in her chest, a tingling in her fingers.

Her reaction scared her. When it came to Jack she felt too much, always had. She shifted, drawing herself up to sit against the bed head, pulling the sheet over her breasts.

'You need to be more specific.'

His eyebrows rose. In surprise because she didn't simply jump at the offer?

His gaze held hers and the intensity of it made her shiver. It wasn't the look of a lover. What she saw, or thought she saw before he shuttered his expression and pulled himself up to sit beside her, was the intense focus Jack always brought to bear on his work. Focus and calculation.

A tiny shiver tracked down her spine.

'I want you to come back to Paris. Come back to me.' He paused, his voice dropping low to a note that spoke of authenticity and emotion.

Yet his expression remained guarded so she couldn't read his feelings.

Because he was so adept at concealing them that it had become second nature?

Or because there were no deeper feelings to conceal?

That possibility froze her mid-breath and she had to focus on dragging in oxygen when her head began to spin.

But the idea shouldn't shock her. After all, that was why she'd fled him in the first place—because the emotional connection had been all on her side, not his.

'You want to continue our affair?'

She didn't imagine the emotion in his expression this time. His frown was real. 'It's not an affair, it's a *marriage*. Doesn't this week prove it's not over? Don't you want more?' He paused. 'I do.'

Bess pressed her hand to her chest as hope and excitement rose so fast her heart galloped.

Of course she wanted more.

She wanted Jack in her bed and in her life. Because despite her best efforts, he was still in her heart.

Could their relationship be mended? Could it be that he'd discovered he had deeper feelings for her?

Jack smiled, that slow, intimate smile that never failed to curl her toes and weaken her resolve.

Instinctively she leaned towards him, drawn by the warmth in his eyes and his admission that he wanted her enough to invite her back into his life. For if she joined him in Paris their reunion would no longer be private.

Shock jolted through Bess as she realised the implications. His invitation proved he wanted to make their relationship work long-term.

Bess knew the world he inhabited. Their separation had ignited endless gossip and press speculation. Her return would spark a similar flurry. Even a man as confident and successful as Jack wouldn't invite that merely for short-term sexual satisfaction.

He was a proud man and the negative press wouldn't have been easy for him, yet in the past five days he hadn't berated her about that. She hadn't let herself read too much into that. Now she couldn't suppress the burgeoning excitement inside.

'I want you *as my wife*. I want you back.'

His smouldering look ignited a fire of longing.

Jack had always been able to make her feel special when they made love. But they weren't making love now. His expression, the husky emotion in his voice and the tension in his body, as if he barely held himself back from sweeping her to him, made Bess feel that nothing mattered to him at this moment but her. That she was his first and only priority.

It was heady for a woman who'd forced herself long ago to accept that her husband didn't love her.

She snapped her mouth shut against the eager words forming on her tongue. How easy to say yes. But this was too important to rush.

Instead she sat back against the pillows, noticing his brows twitch at that tiny withdrawal. 'You think a week of great sex is enough to mend our marriage? You know I want to settle down eventually and have children one day. And there are other things we haven't sorted out. Important things.'

Like the imbalance of love and power between them.

That twitch became a scowl, swiftly gone. But then he'd never been eager to have kids. It was a subject he preferred not to discuss. 'Great sex is a starting point. It proves that there's still a spark between us, something we can build on. And I *did* apologise.'

Bess nodded. He'd apologised for what he'd said on that dreadful night but his words were still branded on her brain.

He'd instructed her not to see Lara. As if she were an employee who'd crossed a corporate line. Normally amenable, Bess had refused and for the first time ever, they'd argued. That was when he'd blurted out that he hadn't married her to attract negative publicity. That he'd married her, among other things, for her pristine reputation. Hanging around with Lara Cartwright would cast an unsavoury shadow over her and by extension him.

Her pristine reputation.

Bess had felt sick to the stomach at the casual way he'd referred to his reason for marrying. Never had Jack been so brutally direct. Before that, he'd been so charming. He'd made a marriage of convenience sound like the most sensible, delightful thing in the world. Especially when he'd made it abundantly clear that he was attracted to her.

'Yes, you said you were sorry. And I know you weren't yourself that night.'

But had it been his rising fever that had made him blurt out such awful things?

Was that what he still thought?

She didn't really know how Jack felt about her now. Physically attracted, yes. But had anything else changed?

How weak she'd been, relishing their sexual compatibility for five whole days and not pressing him about their relationship. Jack hadn't followed through with his offer to talk but she hadn't ventured there either.

She'd been too scared of what she'd hear.

Without giving herself time to think, Bess shoved aside the sheet and shot out of bed, scooping up the silky robe abandoned on the floor and shrugging it on.

'Elisabeth, we need to talk.'

Elisabeth again, not Bess. It was what her father had called her as a child when she'd done something wrong.

It was a tiny thing yet it reminded her that despite the physical intimacy there were still gaping flaws in this relationship. If he'd called her Bess, as he had last night in a voice filled with yearning, she knew her caution would have shattered.

'We absolutely do need to talk, Jack. But not yet. I have to get my head straight first.'

Bess watched him freeze. Saw the staccato jerk of the pulse at his jaw, but then he sat back and nodded. He gave her another smile, a dazzling flash of masculine charm that sent her stomach into free fall and made her knees weak. 'Fair enough. I know, when you think it through, you'll see it makes sense.'

CHAPTER SIX

BESS WISHED SHE had Jack's certainty.

She barely noticed the crystal water frothing warm around her ankles as she meandered up the empty beach, trying to organise her thoughts.

If she returned to Paris she'd be committing anew to a marriage that hadn't worked before. What had really changed?

Jack had apologised for a start. And she'd forgiven him, believing his illness had in part contributed to his insulting ultimatum.

More, and this was huge, he'd altered his packed schedule at a moment's notice just to spend time with her.

He'd put her first. Ahead of business.

Her heart expanded against her ribs and her steps faltered as she remembered that moment. He'd been due to fly out that day, no doubt he'd had back-to-back meetings scheduled for the week, but he'd cancelled them at the last moment to be with her.

Because she was that important to him.

That had been out of character, for Jack was many things but impulsive wasn't one of them.

Her husband—for the first time in ages she allowed herself to think of him that way—was a talented engineer turned ultra-successful entrepreneur. He had a mind like a steel trap, logical, quick and able to strategise so far ahead it made her head spin. He planned everything meticulously, ready for all eventualities. That, with his formidable focus and his first-rate business model, had brought incredible success.

He was the most energetic man she knew and the most daunting. For though he could be kind and charming he *never* acted on impulse. With Jack everything was planned. As for taking time out for fun, that was unheard of. Every social engagement, every event, every appearance fed into his long-term commercial goals. Business was the most important thing in his life.

For Jack to decide on the spur of the moment to forget business simply to be with her...

She stumbled to a halt, her throat thickening. He *must* really care for her. Maybe in her absence he'd realised how much. He'd been so tender with her this week but there'd also been an undercurrent of something else, something that felt almost like desperation. At first she'd assumed it was because they'd been apart so long but as the days progressed that sense of barely leashed urgency had escalated, not abated.

Bess pressed her hand to her suddenly churning stomach. Was it possible Jack was beginning to fall in love with her?

Her breath sawed in her lungs as she struggled for equilibrium. She couldn't assume too much but surely, *surely* there was a chance. She'd go back now and they'd talk properly. If, as seemed likely, Jack's feelings for her were changing, then she'd accept his offer and return to Paris, and try to mend their marriage.

Excitement blazed. She was grinning as she spun around to head back along the beach.

It took a moment to realise someone had called her name. She stopped and looked to her right. There, just a few metres away was a staff member she recognised from reception. Bess hadn't realised she'd walked all the way to the resort's main building.

'I'm sorry to bother you—'

'You're not bothering me. What can I do for you?'

The other woman moved closer, smiling. 'I just wanted to check something, but as Mr Reilly instructed you weren't to be disturbed at your end of the resort I didn't like to call you. It seemed serendipity when I looked up and saw you here.'

Bess frowned. *Jack* had instructed that she not be disturbed? She stiffened, unease trickling down her spine that he'd done so without asking her.

But she ignored it. He'd probably asked for as much privacy as possible and the staff misunderstood. Though now she thought about it she'd seen no-one but him for the past week. The room had been serviced when they were out swimming or sailing. Very occasionally she'd spoken to the waiter bringing or taking away their meals.

She smiled. 'It has been beautifully quiet where we are. I could almost believe there's no-one else staying here.' Which was just as well given the number of times passion had overcome her and Jack on a moonlight walk.

The other woman nodded. 'I'm so pleased. That was the idea when Mr Reilly booked out the other accommodation.'

'I'm sorry, what do you mean?'

The receptionist beamed. 'It was such a lovely romantic gesture. He wanted to reserve the whole resort during your week here so you had complete privacy, but some guests couldn't be persuaded to change their dates. They've been accommodated at the other end of the resort.' She turned and gestured to the other side of the island from where Bess and Jack were staying. When she turned back to Bess her grin vanished, concern replacing her enthusiasm. 'Are you all right?'

Mutely Bess nodded, ignoring her sudden, creeping apprehension. It took a few seconds to find her voice. She chose her words carefully, feeling as if she teetered on a precipice and one wrong word might send her crashing. 'How…' Her voice was a croak. 'How did he manage to do that with no notice?'

The receptionist watched her closely as if realising something was wrong. 'You're right. It wasn't much notice. But your husband was determined and he made it happen in advance of your arrival. I'm so glad you've been enjoying it here.'

Bess nodded. Her smile was a rictus grin as the elation of moments ago bled away. It felt like her blood drained too. She looked down, almost expecting to see the sugar-white sand at her feet stained red.

Jack had planned his stay, *their* stay, before she even arrived?

'So my husband booked his accommodation and booked out half the resort, before we got here?'

The other woman looked bemused but answered readily. 'Yes. Even then it was a huge ask to change so many bookings.'

'I'm sure it was.' But when Jack wanted something he usually got his way.

He'd wanted this week with her and he'd got it. He'd known she'd be here and planned accordingly.

Did it really matter that he planned in advance rather than acted on the spur of the moment? It shouldn't. The fact was he cared enough to want to be with her.

Yet he'd let her believe it was a sudden decision to stay. He'd misled her, saying he was sure the resort could accommodate him, making it sound like he was going to ask to extend his stay whereas he'd already secured the booking.

He still put you first. He spent a whole week ignoring work to be here with you.

The tightness in her chest eased as she drew a relieved breath.

But it's not quite the same, is it, when he'd scheduled it in advance? Instead of making you his top priority, Jack shuffled his schedule to fit you in.

The receptionist was speaking and Bess had to ask her to repeat herself.

'I'm so sorry to bother you with this but I've just discovered an oversight I wanted to clear up. You and Mr Reilly have a booking to leave together by helicopter on Friday but I just noticed you also have a single seat booked to leave on the seaplane the same day. I wanted to check I should cancel the seaplane.'

Jack had already booked for her to leave with him in two days? He was so sure she'd leave with him?

He hadn't even got her answer yet. He'd only just asked her to go to Paris.

Asked or demanded? Now she thought about it, he hadn't framed it as a question.

A sliver of anger pierced her frozen body. He clearly hadn't expected her to need time to think it through. He'd frowned at her withdrawal, then swiftly masked his impatience.

Had he assumed he'd so thoroughly seduced her that she'd meekly go along with his wishes?

Or was she overreacting? What he'd done was no crime and showed he hoped for a positive outcome. Yet this felt too much like the way they'd lived before, Jack always deciding and making arrangements, or having his ultra-efficient staff make arrangements, and Bess acquiescing.

Theirs had been a one-sided marriage in too many ways. If she were to return it would have to be as Jack's equal. Was that what he wanted? Or did he think that with a little time and effort he could persuade her back into their old arrangement?

Nausea stirred. Her head was whirling, her emotions all over the place. She didn't know what to think. Yet beneath her uncertainty was a cold, hard kernel of disappointment and doubt.

The magic had gone out of the morning.

Bess opened the door to Jack's luxurious bungalow and entered, automatically stepping out of her sandals and onto the cool tiled floor. It was time they talked properly.

But as she padded into the vast living space she faltered to a stop. There, dangling from the end of the long lounge, was a scrap of lace. Her bra. She'd worn it yesterday and after dinner Jack had stripped it and the rest of her clothes away and taken her on the lounge.

Her gaze caught a glimpse of turquoise. Her sundress was pooled on the floor half under another lounge. After they'd finished on the lounge Jack had scooped her into his arms and into his bed and she hadn't been back in this room since.

Heat flushed her cheeks. In the bright light of a new day, and the knowledge that he'd planned her seduction, last night's erotic adventures didn't seem quite so wonderful.

She crossed the room, picking up her clothes. And froze when she heard Jack's voice. He must have stepped into the bedroom from the private courtyard. He had his phone on speaker and she recognised the voice of his assistant, Leanne Musgrove.

Bess was trying to decide whether to tell him she was back or leave and return later, when she heard her name mentioned and automatically stilled.

'Will Mrs Reilly need something new to wear to the gala?'

'Good point. It's an important event and it will be her first major appearance in public with me. She'll need something new and spectacular. Make an appointment for the afternoon we return. With the couturier who designed that red velvet for the last Christmas ball. She looked perfect in that.'

A thunderous rush of blood in Bess's ears obliterated the rest of the conversation.

She found herself slumped against the back of the sofa, looking down at the pretty but cheap cotton sundress in her hands. It was serviceable and perfectly appropriate for a woman teaching English as a second language in a hot climate. Or wearing on a relaxed seaside holiday.

It was nothing like the extravagantly expensive wardrobe

Jack had insisted she wear. Would insist she wear if she went back to him.

She blinked, discovering her eyes felt scratchy and her pulse had taken up a strange, out-of-kilter beat. She drew a deep breath.

Jack was so sure of her that he wasn't just making her travel plans. He'd decided what events she'd attend and what she'd wear.

As if she were a mannequin waiting to be dressed in whatever he deemed appropriate!

He wasn't waiting to discuss what she wanted in their relationship. He was forging ahead and deciding for her.

This was even worse than before. At least then he hadn't taken charge of her wardrobe!

Her ears cleared and suddenly she was listening to the conversation in the next room. If only she could make her feet move she wouldn't need to hear any more.

'And I want to move forward the German negotiations now. Check that the presidential suite in Berlin is available from the thirtieth. That will give me time to wrap up everything in Paris.'

Pain shot through Bess's jaw and she realised she'd clenched her molars so tight it felt like she'd crack the enamel.

He'd invited her to Paris but it seemed they wouldn't be staying there. They'd move on to Berlin soon. Because that fitted his business schemes. It didn't matter whether she wanted to live there, much less if she'd prefer a private apartment or house to living in another hotel.

It was the past all over again.

But worse now because she'd actually thought Jack had changed. That he'd missed *her*, not the obedient effigy of a wife he obviously preferred, but a woman with a mind and interests of her own. A woman who, to her regret, had fallen in love with him.

You always were too romantic for your own good.

What other woman, faced with a man who offered marriage in return for paying off her father's debts, would fool herself into believing her convenient husband might one day discover himself in love with her?

It was preposterous. She'd known it for ages.

And still she'd succumbed to the temptation that was Jack Reilly. How smug he must have been when she'd arrived on the island and fallen into his arms and his bed without any effort on his part!

The recollection made her feel cheap.

Tainted.

She dropped her dress and bra and turned away. She didn't want anything Jack Reilly had touched.

He was still talking to Leanne, the woman who'd once bombarded her with schedules of how she was expected to spend her time. He was welcome to her! Maybe he could take her on next to fill the vacancy of wife when Bess left this time.

Bess reached the front door, scooped up her sandals and stepped outside, not bothering to put them on. All she wanted was to get away from here as fast as possible. She had a single suitcase to pack and with luck might be able to get a flight out this morning.

She'd text Jack when she'd gone, tell him that she'd realised the passion they'd shared wasn't enough and she had to move on. Maybe it was cowardly, not confronting him now. She wanted to, so badly. But she knew she'd never be able to do it and maintain her dignity. The hurt was so bad, the sense of betrayal so deep, she'd end up shouting and raging, or worse, in tears. She refused to let him see her like that.

A raw, unguarded sound escaped her mouth. She told herself it was laughter. For here she was, running away from her husband a second time because she hadn't managed to do it properly before.

That was better than admitting it was a groan of visceral pain. Because the truth about Jack's feelings for her, or lack of them, rent her heart, her self-esteem, her very soul apart.

CHAPTER SEVEN

BESS STARED AT the picture on the opposite wall. It showed a woman, head bent and hair falling forward to curtain her face, tenderly cradling her baby bump. She couldn't tear her eyes away from it.

'I take it this wasn't the news you were hoping for.'

She met the doctor's enquiring eyes.

Had she been hoping for different news? This meant her life would change forever. At a time when she already felt it had spun out of control.

But now her suspicions had been confirmed, she didn't know how she felt. 'I'm just finding it hard to believe it's true. I almost didn't make this appointment because it seemed impossible.'

Though given the number of times she and Jack had had sex in that week together, logic told her it was far from impossible, especially as she'd stopped taking the pill when she left Paris and they'd relied only on condoms.

Jack had always been meticulous about protection. He'd made it clear from the first that he wasn't ready to start a family.

Her lips twisted. It seemed that was one thing the mighty Jack Reilly couldn't control.

The doctor's smile was reassuring. 'Many women feel that way, especially the first time. It's a lot to take in.'

Bess nodded. She'd had weeks to get used to this possibility but still it felt like she'd wake up to find it had all been a dream. That's why, instead of going to a GP for confirmation of the home test she'd taken, Bess had accepted her flatmate's offer to get her an appointment with her sister, an obstetrician. Receiving the news from the specialist left no room for doubt.

She'd never imagined an unplanned pregnancy. She felt healthy but what if she'd picked up some so-far-unnoticed health issue from her travels? Something that might affect a baby?

'I don't feel different. No morning sickness, my breasts don't feel sensitive, nothing.'

Just that all-important missed period.

The doctor's smile grew. 'That's not uncommon at this stage, and lots of women don't get morning sickness. Time will tell. The good news is that everything seems normal. No indications at this stage of anything to worry about.' She paused, her gaze searching. 'I can refer you to a counselling service if you'd like. And I'll give you some information on nutrition, diet and so forth, as well as book you in for a follow-up appointment.'

The rest of the consultation passed in a blur. Bess asked questions but only took in half the answers. Her head was spinning and everything felt unreal.

Leaving the building, she paused on the footpath, looking at the London street with new eyes. The scents of traffic and rain-wet pavement hit her nostrils. The hiss of a taxi's tyres sounded loud as it passed and the red flowers in a nearby window box glowed vibrantly. It felt like all her senses were heightened.

From shock? Excitement? She barely knew.

Bess inhaled slowly. One thing she did know was that she'd have to tell Jack. He deserved to know he was going to be a father. But that could wait a little. There was no rush since she knew he wouldn't be thrilled. She wasn't up to dealing with him just yet.

Maybe the shock was wearing off for, despite the wreck of her marriage and the fact that she'd undoubtedly be a single mother since Jack wasn't interested in a family, she felt a tickle of excitement.

Her blood fizzed in her veins.

She was going to have a baby.

She'd always wanted to have children one day. She'd been prepared to wait because Jack hadn't been ready and besides, she'd wanted to pursue the career she loved. But some things came in their own time. She'd have to find a way to work her career around the baby. But other women did it, so why shouldn't she?

Bess turned and headed towards the Tube station. She had a lot of thinking and planning to do.

Jack was in a foul mood.

Nothing had gone right since his return to Paris.

A major deal that had been months in the making looked like falling through and he couldn't gather the energy to mount an aggressive campaign to save it.

He had energy to burn, spending long hours in the private gym of the presidential suite, pounding the pavements of Paris in the dawn light or doing a little sparring practice at a nearby boxing gym. But somehow he couldn't translate that energy into productive work.

Meetings were a trial, concentration was difficult and it took all his self-control not to snap at staff who were used to following his lead rather than coming up with innovative solutions to problems themselves.

It was his own fault. He employed the best but in the past he'd insisted on the final say in every major negotiation, every new direction. In the eight weeks since he'd been back in Paris he'd learned the hard way that his approach to business, effective as it had been until now, was too reliant on him taking an active role. He needed to delegate more. *Was* delegating more, and some of his staff, while excellent at following orders, struggled to come up to the mark.

He needed to find time for mentoring, training and extra recruitment. He needed to focus on his plans for the move to Berlin that he'd delayed again but couldn't put off much longer. He needed to find a solution to the problems that looked like sending his newest scheme into mothballs.

Instead he found himself thinking about Elisabeth. Again.

He couldn't get the woman out of his mind. The sleek softness of her skin, the gentle sound of her breathing in the night as she snuggled against him, the fire in her amber eyes when they found heaven together.

He shot to his feet and stalked the length of his office, noticing for the first time that he really wasn't fond of the ornate antique desk or the gilt-edged sideboard. Or the too-formal arrangement of flowers on the low table between the priceless sofas. It was one of the downsides of staying in a hotel, even one of this superb calibre, that he lived with someone else's decorative choices.

Jack frowned. In the past he'd barely noticed the furnishings. His staff in Paris worked from a permanent office but he mainly worked remotely from his hotel.

It was just that he'd been here too long. He'd meant to leave Paris much earlier.

Since Elisabeth left he hadn't been able to move on.

He sucked in a sharp breath, feeling that dagger-sharp slice through his gut again.

Twice now she'd done that, once here and once in the Caribbean, and still the pain hadn't eased. He'd told himself it was wounded pride he felt but he wasn't that naïve. It was far, far more. Far more even than fury.

His wife had damaged him in a way he still found difficult to believe. Especially since he'd assumed, after she fell so eagerly into his bed again, that she'd realised her mistake in leaving and would come back once he'd apologised. He'd planned to make things up to her, schedule more time with her, not just at work-related events. Make sure she knew how he valued her. Make her feel special.

But he hadn't had her measure at all.

He'd been stunned when she'd left again. Stunned, angry and gutted. The message she'd left had made it clear she never wanted to see him. Since then he hadn't been able to reach her and his pride had stopped him setting an investigator to find her. He wasn't going to run after her, begging for attention.

Elisabeth's defection brought back memories he'd spent his life suppressing. Of his parents' lack of interest. Their total absorption in their passionate, poisonous, on-again-off-again relationship to the exclusion of all else, including their only child.

He was lucky his grandmother had intervened to raise him. She'd had little choice after he'd turned up on her door after midnight, barefoot and in his pyjamas, shivering with distress. It was either her or foster care.

Jack stalked to the too-ornate sideboard and chose a Baccarat crystal brandy balloon. He was reaching for the cognac when one of those ancient memories stopped him.

He flinched, remembering the sound of splintering glass. His father's rage as he surveyed the glittering shards from the glass that had been thrown at him, and the stain of spreading liquor on polished floorboards. The fury in his eyes as he'd stalked over to Jack's mother, who wore black satin and a challenging pout.

Jack couldn't recall what the disagreement had been about that time. His mother's spending or his father's long hours at work? Or had one found out the other in an affair? They were both serially unfaithful but could never finally break the bond between them, always returning to their tempestuous marriage.

For the longest time it looked like there'd be violence that night. His father's hands hadn't been gentle but nor had his mother's. Jack, who'd come to the lounge room to say goodnight before going to bed, had stood aghast, his bedraggled toy lion pressed against his puny chest as he watched his father's big hands wrap around his mother's delicate neck. He'd tilted up her chin, growling deep from the back of his throat and making every hair on Jack's body stand on end.

Jack had been gathering the courage to call out and try to stop them when his father jerked her close and kissed her with a ferocity that terrified a child of six. He'd been frightened too by the sound of tearing fabric, until his mother laughed that husky, taunting laugh she saved only for his father and dragged her long nails slowly and deliberately down his neck.

Jack blinked and put down the glass. He didn't want alcohol. He preferred to be in full possession of his faculties.

He didn't like anything that made him weak or threatened his control. After his early experiences he'd made it his mission to control whatever situation he found himself in. Not to be buffeted by unruly emotions or unwanted surprises. He worked out what he wanted, assessed how to get it, planned meticulously and acted decisively.

He wasn't weak or volatile like his parents.

His thoughts slewed to Elisabeth and how spectacularly he'd misjudged her. She didn't make him feel weak. On the contrary, with her he was always aware of his vigour and the potency of his desire. But volatile? He frowned, reluctantly admitting that exactly described his feelings for his wife.

Soon to be ex-wife if she proceeded with the divorce she threatened.

Jack's fingers curled into fists, his blood rushing faster at the thought. Even now, he couldn't bring himself to contemplate that. Because he always finished what he started? Because he wasn't ready to end their marriage? Because he didn't like ceding power?

His phone rang and he was tempted to ignore it. But he hadn't got where he was by ignoring potentially important calls. He checked the number. Leanne.

'Yes?'

'We have a situation.'

Jack pinched the bridge of his nose. Another complication? He was tempted to walk away from this latest French deal and cut his losses. 'What does the Count want now?'

'It's not business.' His PA paused long enough to make him wonder how bad this situation was. 'It's your wife.'

Sweat broke out across his brow and his stomach plunged sickeningly. 'Elisabeth? Is she all right? What's happened to her?'

'She's fine,' Leanne hurriedly reassured. 'As far as I can tell. It's just…'

Her unaccustomed hesitation fed deepening anxiety. That was a revelation. Jack had never been a worrier, not since leaving his parents' home and discovering that with hard work and planning, and no unruly emotional attachments, life didn't need to be chaotic or tempestuous.

'Sorry. Social media has been going wild. Stories are starting to circulate and the paparazzi have photos.'

Jack's mouth flattened. 'From the Caribbean?'

Just what he needed! He'd faced down unending gossip over the state of his marriage and his missing wife. After the recent debacle when Elisabeth had run out on him *again*, it had been a small comfort to know that at least that hadn't played out under the eyes of the world's press.

Anger stirred anew. Elisabeth had a lot to answer for.

'One photo from the Caribbean but others as well, of Mrs

Reilly. I've sent some links through to you and I need to warn you—'

'No need, Leanne.' He might be furious and the timing might be lousy, but he'd dealt with plenty of press speculation in the past. 'I'll check them out and let you know if I want anything done about it.'

He ended the call and found the links she'd sent.

Slowly Jack sank into the chair he'd left, intent on his phone as everything seemed to slow, the thud of his heart, his breathing, even his thoughts.

The press had got hold of a photo of him and Elisabeth during their week together. It was taken at a distance when they'd been out for the day on a yacht. But even from a distance it was obvious from their body language that there was nothing platonic about their reunion. The way he leaned over her spoke of protectiveness and raw physical need. Her graceful neck was arched up, her lips parted as she looked up at him.

Jack's heart quickened. They looked in thrall to each other, as if nothing else existed but the pair of them. As if Elisabeth couldn't bear even the tiny distance between them.

He grunted with sour laughter. How a photo could lie.

He scanned his own expression and told himself he didn't look bewitched or protective. It had been simple lust.

Grimacing, he scanned the text that rhapsodised about their secret reunion. 'Sex in the Sand' was a tawdry headline and he could only thank his lucky stars they hadn't managed a photo of the times he and Elisabeth had made love on a beach. The only question was why the photo hadn't appeared weeks before.

Then his heart stopped. The next photo was of Elisabeth stepping out onto a city street. Behind her was a glossy black door with a fanlight window above and a discreet brass plaque beside it. Helpfully, the photographer had provided a close-up of the plaque. It gave the name of the doctor, an obstetrician.

Jack's fingers felt numb and he almost dropped the phone.

An obstetrician? Not a gynaecologist but a doctor who specialised in delivering babies.

Elisabeth, pregnant?

She couldn't be. Yet, remembering how they hadn't been able to keep their hands off each other, technically it was all too possible.

But he'd been meticulous about using condoms.

Did that mean the baby, if there was one, wasn't his? His gut spasmed with nausea at the idea of her going from his bed to another man's.

No, he refused to believe it.

His breathing eased and the tang of bile at the back of his throat abated as sense reasserted itself. Elisabeth was discriminating. He'd been her only lover and he couldn't believe she'd have gone from him straight to someone else.

So any pregnancy meant it was his child.

His mouth dried as shock blasted him like impact waves from an explosion. His brain almost atrophied at the idea of a baby, *his* baby. The notion was too big, too foreign to absorb straightaway.

For a long moment he found himself staring at the ugly antique desk, just trying to catch his breath.

Then he made himself read on.

What followed was a sickening ramble of conjecture. The reporter explained how long Jack and Elisabeth had been separated, noting that 'Mrs Reilly had been travelling internationally since and it was unknown if she'd travelled alone.' They hinted she'd had an affair.

Jack growled through gritted teeth, his hackles rising.

Then came speculation about the 'secret sex romp in the Caribbean' and more shots of Elisabeth in London, clearly unaware that she was the target of paparazzi lenses. There were close-ups of her trim figure and breathless discussion of whether she might be pregnant to him or someone else, or perhaps investigating fertility treatment and whether she intended to be a single mother.

Jack closed the piece and clicked another link. This article claimed she was definitely pregnant with his baby. There were more photos of Elisabeth, this time looking startled and afraid, one hand raised as if to ward off the photographer.

Swearing, Jack put the phone down. His hand was rock steady but his breath was laboured and his chest cramped as if his lungs were caught in a vice.

Elisabeth pregnant.

Pregnant with his child.

His gut churned. He'd known all his life that he didn't want to pass his genes to another generation. Given the disaster his own parents had been he didn't want to take that chance. No child deserved such criminal negligence. As role models they'd been perfect examples of what parents shouldn't be, utterly self-absorbed, unreliable and irresponsible to the point of being dangerous. Not that they'd intended to hurt him—he simply hadn't figured in their thinking.

He'd done his best to be as different from them as he could be. Yet, despite the satisfaction of knowing he shared few character traits with them, his secret fear was that, in the wrong circumstances, he'd reveal an unruly, passionate, irrational side.

No wonder the feelings Elisabeth evoked made him wary. For there was nothing considered or rational about what she made him feel. The sheer depth of his need for her, the way his hunger grew and grew instead of easing, hinted at appetites he couldn't manage.

His parents' example was one of the reasons he'd been attracted to a convenient marriage that melded business goals and sexual satisfaction rather than fall into the trap of so-called love.

Maybe you don't have a choice about becoming a father. Maybe it's out of your control.

He shuddered. He'd spent his life working to make his world fit his needs. To manage every contingency. It was the way he'd learned to survive. But now…

Was Elisabeth really pregnant? He tried and failed to think of another reason she'd visit a Harley Street obstetrician.

He looked again at his phone, pain and fury scouring his belly at her expression in that last photo. She looked dismayed and fragile as she faced the photographer invading her personal space.

Jack shot to his feet, his thumb punching speed dial.

'I need my wife's address in London,' he said when Leanne picked up. 'And cancel all my appointments.'

CHAPTER EIGHT

'I'M SORRY, BESS, I really am. But I've got no choice in the circumstances.'

She looked into Janusz's earnest brown eyes and nodded. Her heart sank because he was right, this couldn't continue. 'Of course. I understand.'

Her boss, no, make that her now ex-boss, paced to the window, shot an indignant look down into the street, then returned to his desk and sat down opposite her.

'Those vultures. They don't give a damn what damage they're causing to you or anyone else.' He shook his head. 'All this time we've been wanting publicity to get more donations. But not this sort of publicity.'

Bess clasped her hands together. 'I'm sorry, Janusz. I thought I'd managed to shake them off. I didn't see anyone following me on the way to work.'

'It's not your fault. You're the victim. It's just that a lot of our clients have been victims too and still carry the scars. Being jostled and shouted at by predatory photographers when they try to come in the door is disastrous. A lot of people haven't even shown up today.'

Bess slumped in her seat. No matter what he said, she'd brought this on.

The charity did a fantastic job with limited funds, supporting migrants and especially refugees, many of whom had been through severe trauma, even torture. She'd been so pleased to get a job here teaching English. But now innocent people, with problems far greater than hers, were running scared because of the press pack camped outside.

She pressed a hand to her stomach as nausea stirred. Morning sickness or distress?

'Maybe if this all dies down,' he read her expression and amended, '*when* it dies down, you could come back.'

Bess nodded but she didn't believe that would happen. Not completely.

Maybe if she and Jack were still the picture-perfect husband and wife, raising their child together, the attention would wear off. But if they were together she couldn't imagine Jack curtailing his plans for commercial world domination long enough to let her pursue a meaningful career. In other circumstances the idea would almost be funny.

She had an awful feeling that the press intended to hound her indefinitely. People were fascinated by Jack, who made lists of the world's rich and sexy on a regular basis. In the last year the pair of them had become notorious as the glamour couple who'd split under mysterious circumstances. She was the woman who'd said no to Jack Reilly's potent brand of looks, power, charisma and wealth when so many others found him irresistible. Now the media clamoured for a story.

She winced, imagining regular press updates on her pregnancy. No doubt things would become even more difficult when the baby was born.

She sank back in the hard seat and wondered if there was any way out of this.

'Thanks, Janusz. Maybe one day. Meanwhile, the sooner I leave the sooner you can all get back to normal.' She got to her feet, feeling weary beyond her years.

'I'll come with you. You'll need help getting out of the building.' He ushered her from the room and down the stairs. 'I think we'd better order a taxi.'

He was right. As they headed towards the lobby the noise

outside grew and Bess faltered back against his guiding hand. She wasn't afraid of crowds but these people were ravening wolves.

'Elisabeth.'

She jumped and turned towards the back of the lobby where the centre's new counsellor, Zoe, stood talking with a tall, familiar figure.

Bess blinked, trying to reconcile what her eyes told her with what she knew to be impossible. That powerful, rangy figure couldn't be Jack Reilly. Jack was in Europe attending to his all-important business. He couldn't be here in a slightly ramshackle building in a run-down part of London.

Then he stepped forward into the light and the air rushed from her lungs. No other man melded urbane sophistication, raw masculinity and an aura of power in such a high-octane mix.

Her stomach tightened as her breath seized.

'Jack Reilly. Elisabeth's husband.' He held his hand out to Janusz. 'You must be the centre's director.'

Janusz said something, Bess wasn't sure what because shock and the rush of blood in her ears made the scene take on an unreal quality.

She read the men's grave expressions, saw them speak and nod as if an agreement then heard Jack say, 'I'll take care of things from here. Elisabeth will be safe with me. The sooner we leave the better.'

That jolted her brain into gear. Her blood pressure skyrocketed. He'd only been here a minute and already he was issuing orders.

She was sick of him taking over her life, making decisions that should be hers.

'No-one asked you to take care of things, Jack. I'll make my own way out.' His appearance had just set the seal on this hellish day.

From her peripheral vision she saw Janusz frown. He even

opened his mouth as if to protest but Jack beat him to it. Naturally.

'Of course, Elisabeth. If you really want to.' Her husband stepped to one side and in the silence she heard anew the awful hubbub outside. Then the front door opened and one of the administrative staff hurried in, looking harried, and slammed it shut. She slumped back against the door, grimacing.

'Or,' Jack said softly, 'I could get you away from here so they don't follow.'

Bess looked from Janusz to Zoe then across to the young admin assistant and her chest cramped. What had she been thinking, putting her pride first when everyone else here was bearing the brunt of this disastrous situation because of her?

She breathed deep and made herself face her nemesis. To his credit he didn't look in the least smug. In fact, if she had to try deciphering his bland expression she'd be tempted to say he looked on edge. But she knew that wasn't true. Jack Reilly was full of confidence and by the sound of it he already had an escape plan.

Bess drew herself up to her full height. 'Thank you, Jack. That would be very helpful.' She turned to the others. 'Again, I'm so very sorry to bring all this down on you.'

'Nonsense,' said Zoe. 'You've nothing to apologise for. Besides.' She shrugged. 'Some of us have come up with a way of capitalising on that lot out there.' She held up a large piece of cardboard with the name of the centre in capitals and below it in red the words *Donate Now* followed by the charity's phone number. 'We thought one for each front window.'

Janusz nodded and smiled and Jack took out his phone to copy down the number. 'Great idea. And to make up a little for all this inconvenience, I'll have my assistant ring through to organise a donation.' He named a sum that had the others reeling in shock.

Bess was torn between pleasure at the thoughtful gesture

and annoyance that Jack's wealth allowed him to deal with most of life's problems so easily.

He never let anything get under his skin. If he had a problem he simply strategised a way out of it.

How is he going to strategise his way out of fatherhood?

Bess had no doubt that was his aim. He'd made it clear that he wasn't contemplating a family any time soon and therefore she shouldn't either.

Her heart dipped. Was he here to pay her off and ensure that she and their child never bothered him again? Would he suggest a termination?

Once again her stomach churned with nausea.

Before they'd married, and in the early days after that, she'd fooled herself into thinking one day he'd fall in love with her. In her fantasies, having Jack's baby had been one more highlight in the wonderful life they would share together.

Instead they were trapped in a draughty hall with a pack of photographers outside, baying for attention.

She caught Jack's gaze. Far from being ardent, his expression made her remember a documentary about a bomb specialist about to try defusing a land mine. Wariness, calculation and coolness. That's what she'd seen in his eyes and what she recognised now in Jack.

Had she really expected warmth or tenderness?

She shut her eyes, shivering as the nausea intensified.

A hand closed around her upper arm. She would have known his touch blindfolded because of her body's response. That little thrill of pleasure, the hitch in her breathing, the warmth that spread from his touch.

Bess swallowed hard, feeling the absurd rush of wetness against her lashes. She hated her weakness for this man and despised herself for it.

That attraction should be dead. His behaviour should have killed it, his machinations, his deliberate plan to seduce her then put her back in that gilded box where he made every decision and she was mere window dressing.

'Elisabeth. Bess.' His voice dropped to a whisper only she could hear. To her disordered senses it sounded as if he were in pain too. 'Trust me. You're safe, I won't let them hurt you.'

It wasn't the paparazzi she feared.

It was him, or more accurately, herself. Her eyes snapped open and he was close, close enough to kiss, leaning down with a frown on his face. Even now she imagined tenderness in those impossibly blue eyes and that whisky-and-honey voice.

That wouldn't do. She couldn't allow such self-delusion.

Bess blinked back the unwanted tears and stiffened her spine. She conjured up the smile her mother had taught her so she could appear delighted even when bored by the conversation at some formal event.

It was the smile she'd perfected following her mother's death when her father had relied on her so much. A smile tested when, a bare year later, her dad remarried, to a woman who barely tolerated Bess. A smile that had become second nature through her own marriage as her so-called social life deteriorated into a PR exercise for her husband's business.

'Of course they won't hurt me. They're just after photos and maybe an unguarded word.'

She shifted her weight, slipping her arm free, watching a knot form on his forehead as if he didn't like her stepping away.

He should be used to it by now.

Bess turned to address the others. 'Thank you for everything. I've so enjoyed working here. I hope, with me gone, things will quieten down.' She nodded in response to their good wishes and moved towards the front door.

'Not that way.'

This time Jack didn't touch her, but he moved to stand between her and the entrance.

At her raised eyebrows he nodded towards the back of the

building. 'As soon as you're ready I'll have a decoy limo pull up at the front with a couple of security staff to clear a path. That will keep the press occupied.' He pulled his phone out again. 'Meanwhile we'll go out the back where I have a driver waiting.'

Bess imagined being swept away in an anonymous car, leaving the melee of photographers behind, and some of the tension binding her rigid muscles eased. Her smile was instantaneous and real. 'Good thinking. Thank you.'

Minutes later their car pulled out into the back street and, via a roundabout route, onto a main road heading away from the centre. No-one seemed to notice them go and they weren't tailed.

Bess let out a sigh of relief. She kept her face averted from the window, reducing the chance of being spotted from the street. Which meant she couldn't avoid Jack on the back seat beside her, or the growing claustrophobia from being too close to this man who made her feel too much. Her skin felt too tight and her breath too shallow. Her quickened pulse had less to do with the press pack than with being near him.

'How long have you known him?'

Jack's question confused her. 'Sorry, who do you mean?'

'The centre's director.'

His expression was almost blank, giving little away. Yet maybe he wasn't as good at hiding his thoughts as before, or perhaps now the blinkers had been stripped from her eyes, Bess could read him a little better. Despite his calm demeanour and the lazy stretch of his legs, there was a tension in him that hadn't been there when they'd discussed avoiding the paparazzi.

Her brow knotted. 'Janusz?'

A muscle in Jack's jaw flexed hard. 'That's him.'

She paused, wondering what had got under Jack's skin. Something had. She felt his tension. 'Not long, only since I started work there. Why?'

* * *

Jack looked into those cognac eyes and felt something shift hard inside him.

He'd been prepared to deal with pushy photographers and a recalcitrant wife. What he hadn't been ready for was the jealousy that knifed him as he'd watched Elisabeth walk down the stairs with another man's hand on her back. Elisabeth starting in distress at the sight of Jack and shrinking back against that other man as if he'd protect her from her husband.

She'd stiffened in rejection when Jack touched her. As if his very touch hurt.

His gut roiled at the idea of her leaning on some man other than him. *Preferring* that man.

Jealousy had been a searing stab to the belly. It was a new experience. During their time together he'd been so sure of his wife's affection and loyalty that he'd basked in a warm glow of satisfaction and pride.

Now he just had to see her obvious regard for another man to feel worried and wrong inside.

He cleared his throat, aiming for a neutral tone. Even so the words grazed his larynx like broken glass against bare skin. 'You seem close.'

'Not really. But I like him and he's very good at what he does. That's one of the reasons the centre's so effective. People trust him and he doesn't let them down.'

Was that a crack at him? Jack stiffened, until he saw her curiosity. 'Are you wondering about your donation? Believe me, the money will be put to excellent use.'

He drew a deep breath, trying to find his equilibrium. 'That's good to know.' As if he cared about that when all his concern centred on her.

The intensity of his feelings rocked him. Ever since he'd seen that photo of her, shrinking back from a photographer on the street, it felt like he hadn't been able to draw a proper breath.

Elisabeth shrugged and looked out at the street as if dismissing him. But an instant later her gaze locked on his. 'This isn't the way to my place.' She made it sound like an accusation.

'No. That's the first place they'll look once they realise you've gone.'

She was already shaking her head. 'I want to go home. How do I lower this privacy screen and talk to the driver?'

'Going home is the last thing you want to do. You'll be mobbed and—'

It was as if he'd flicked a switch. In an instant she turned from contained politeness to raging fury. Colour flushed her cheeks and her eyes glittered. She didn't raise her voice but it vibrated with such emotion he felt it smash against him. 'Don't you *dare* tell me what I want, Jack Reilly. I've had more than enough of you telling me what to do!'

Her chin lifted, her jaw setting mutinously, and he regretted putting his foot in it. Yet at the same time something within him sparked into life.

In the Caribbean they'd connected in ways they hadn't before. Everything had felt more vital, more *real*, as they opened up to the passion that had always run strongly, yet within defined boundaries, between them.

Now, for the first time today, he felt like he'd found that passionate, strong woman again. He didn't give a damn about her spiky anger. Better that than having her shrink from him. Or try to blank him with that bland stare.

How he'd missed her.

He'd happily argue with her all day if it meant making up with her tonight.

But she didn't feel the same. Reading the scorn she didn't bother to hide, he felt something shrivel within him. He blinked. She wasn't just angry but contemptuous too.

He spoke slowly, grappling with that. 'I'm trying to protect you, Elisabeth.'

She shook her head so vehemently, her dark ponytail lashed

around her shoulders. 'It doesn't matter what you're trying to do. I won't accept that excuse. Ever since we met, ever since we married, you've made every decision, expecting me to follow wherever you lead. But I'm not accepting that anymore, Jack. From now on I make my own decisions.'

Jack stared. 'Excuse? I don't need an excuse to try to protect my wife.' Didn't she understand he had her best interests in mind?

'I prefer to protect myself. And to make my own decisions rather than be dictated to.' Her belligerent stare was a direct provocation.

As if *he* were the enemy here, rather than the one running interference between her and the paparazzi. His heart raced and his stomach churned, rejecting the idea. Leaden silence settled as he took that in.

'You really want to go to your flat?'

He'd seen a photo of the place. Insufficient security. Minimal escape routes to escape the photographers.

She folded her arms over her chest. 'I do.'

Jack pressed the intercom and spoke to the driver. 'A change of direction.' He gave Elisabeth's address, watching her eyes widen as she realised he knew where she lived.

'You never told me.'

Her mouth flattened. 'Never told you what?'

'That you don't like me protecting you. Being decisive and—'

'It's more than being decisive. It's not respecting me enough to make my own decisions, and I did tell you, in Paris.'

Jack scowled, searching his memory and crossing his own arms, mirroring her combative attitude. He felt combative himself. He'd been accused of many things but never of bullying women. That would be too much like his father's behaviour and one thing he'd always prided himself on was how different he was to his old man.

'I don't recall any such complaint.'

She rolled her eyes. 'The night you told me you'd married me for my pristine reputation and you didn't want it marred by my friendship with Lara.'

'I have no recollection of you saying that.'

That night was a blur of pain. He had minimal recall except of his blinding headache, annoyance that the evening had gone badly and an expression on his wife's face that he'd never seen before, one he never hoped to see again. Distress combined with hurt and anger.

She stared as if trying to read the truth in his face. Slowly he shook his head. 'I'm not lying, Elisabeth. I've never lied to you.' He let that sink in before continuing. 'Whatever it was you accused me of that night, I didn't take it in. Nor,' he added, impatience building, 'did you tell me this in the Caribbean.'

His molars clenched as he recalled her abrupt departure, just when he thought things were finally right, better than right, between them. 'Instead of running away, *twice*, you could have done me the courtesy of explaining.'

Colour flushed her cheeks and throat. 'I did explain in my text. That physical passion isn't enough for me. You and I want different things in a marriage. That's what matters.' When he didn't say anything she went on. 'I heard you on the phone that day to Leanne, planning our return to Paris and a move to Berlin, even organising what I should wear. But I'm not a doll to be dressed up and paraded around. I'm a *woman*!'

As if he wasn't fully aware of that fact.

Even bristling with negative energy, and with her every word widening the gap between them, Elisabeth's femininity spoke on the most primal level to the most masculine part of him. He wanted her, not just sexually, but in ways he couldn't explain.

The enormity of that need was what had brought him from Paris to rescue her. That and the connection between them that he *knew* still existed, despite her furious words.

He still wanted to rescue her, though she looked as if she'd like to bury him.

Too bad. They had things to discuss, important things, like the child she might be carrying. His pulse quickened on the thought, but this wasn't the place for that discussion.

'If you'd stayed around to talk I would have explained that I was trying to make things easier for you.' He paused, holding her gaze. 'I didn't want you stressed trying to prepare in such a tight timeframe for such a prestigious event with all the world's eyes on us. You missed the worst of the press attention while you were gallivanting off to Africa and Asia, but the gossip was relentless and brutal. I thought it my duty, if you came back with me,' his voice grew rough, 'to shield you as much as possible. At least to give you the armour of a fabulous couture outfit for the occasion.'

Her eyes widened and for a moment he'd almost swear he'd taken her by surprise. But instead of accepting his word she tightened her mouth and looked away. When she turned back her expression was so devoid of warmth he felt a chill skate across his bones.

'That's no excuse. There's a difference between assistance and taking over. I spent all our marriage fitting in with whatever it was you wanted.' Her expression was strained and so unutterably weary it sucked the fight out of him. 'That's not for me, Jack. I thought I could handle it but I can't. Not anymore.'

Jack felt his breath snare in his lungs and had that panicked sensation he recalled from childhood, that he couldn't breathe. Tight bands crushed his chest but it wasn't the lack of oxygen that worried him so much as the crashing sense of failure.

Dismay gripped him, and a kaleidoscope of fragmented memories bombarded him. Of the many times as a kid when he hadn't been good enough or important enough to win his parents' attention much less approval. Of how he hadn't been able to make them care or even just stay with him.

He'd told himself the problem had been with them, not himself.

Had he been wrong? Was he tainted with some fatal flaw?

Jack gritted his teeth. If he had one core quality it was determination. Sheer obstinacy had seen him rise above the vagaries of his early life and make something of himself. That determination to make a positive mark in the world, as well as make money, had been behind the success of his business. Determination had won him this alluring, intriguing woman and it would get her back. He vowed it.

The car turned into a narrow residential road with lines of parked cars on either side. The three-story houses here had been broken up into flats, all the same. But halfway down the street one stood out from the rest because of the people clustered on the pavement.

He pressed the intercom. 'Slow down a little.' He turned to Elisabeth. 'Are you ready to confront that mob?'

The footpath was so full that a woman with a pram had to walk out onto the road to pass. From a first-floor window he saw a dismayed face pressed against the glass for a moment before it disappeared. If he wasn't mistaken that was Elisabeth's flat.

'Your flatmate doesn't look impressed.'

His wife sent him a fulminating glare then bit her lip. 'Can you blame her? This is a nightmare. She can't go out without being pestered.'

'And you want to go back there and add to the furore?'

For a moment she was silent then she sighed and slumped back in her seat. 'Okay. You win. Take me to a hotel while I call my flatmate and explain.'

Jack gave directions to the driver who turned at the next intersection and took them smartly away from the area.

Today had brought unexpected insights from Elisabeth. Disturbing insights.

But knowledge was power. At least now he knew why she'd walked out on him.

And brutal as it was, this situation with the press meant she had to stop running from him.

Jack felt a flicker of excitement ignite. He could work with that.

CHAPTER NINE

'So, TALK TO ME, ELISABETH.'

Bess looked up from her contemplation of the manicured private garden at the back of the gracious London town house. She managed not to wince as she met Jack's assessing stare. Despite his relaxed demeanour, sprawled in an armchair across from hers, his eyes were laser bright.

He'd been silent since he'd won the argument about her not returning to her flat, only speaking to give their driver a new address, then introduce her to the housekeeper who opened the glossy black door of this gorgeous mansion in a part of London favoured by the very rich.

He hadn't explained whose house this was, nor did she ask. She had more important questions on her mind. Like where she was going to go while her flat was a magnet for photographers. And how she'd support herself now she'd lost her job.

Bess looked down at the porcelain teacup in her hand and found it empty. She couldn't even remember drinking the tea. She put it down on an antique side table, then wished she hadn't because she didn't know what to do with her hands.

'Thank you for rescuing me, Jack. You were right.' How it went against the grain to admit that. 'I didn't have a plan to deal with the press. I find this whole situation overwhelming.'

His expression softened. 'Anyone would find it overwhelming, even frightening.'

Yes, frightening. That was the word. She wasn't merely annoyed, flustered and indignant, but scared.

It was only now that she was safe, at least temporarily, from the press pack that she realised how scared she'd been. There was a fine tremor in her hands and her shoulders bunched high and tight.

He might have read her mind. 'You're completely safe here. You have my promise that I won't leave you to cope with that sort of aggressive behaviour alone.'

The gratitude that filled her was immense, until she realised her predicament. How could she accept protection from the man she was determined to cut from her life?

'Thanks. I appreciate it, but—'

Jack raised his hand to stop her protest. 'No arguments about this at least. You're still my wife and even if you weren't, do you really think I'm the sort of man to turn my back on someone being hounded so brutally?'

Bess snapped her mouth shut.

She'd spent so long dwelling on Jack's flaws she'd forgotten the other side to his character.

He hadn't hesitated to step in when they'd taken a short-cut down an alley a year ago and come across a distressed woman being pressed up against a wall by an abusive man. When words hadn't worked, Jack had physically pulled the man away. There'd been a scuffle, and to this day Bess was sure she'd seen the glint of a knife in the other man's hand, but in a few quick moves Jack had disarmed him and bundled him away while she supported the crying woman.

Then there was the time they'd dined at a renowned Parisian restaurant and witnessed a young waiter's distress after spilling food over a client. It hadn't been his fault for another diner had barged into him. But as they were leaving, they'd overheard a staff member whispering that the waiter had been sacked. Jack had made it his business to recommend the young man to a celebrity chef acquaintance who was opening a new restaurant.

Her husband was good at rescuing people.

Except, she reminded herself, she only needed rescuing from *him*. Or more precisely, herself and her treacherous emotions.

She met his stare and nodded. 'I appreciate the breathing space while I decide what to do next.' Because she'd lost her job and, at least temporarily, her home. She felt utterly adrift. It would take a while to regroup.

Jack opened his mouth as if to speak, perhaps tell her what she should do next, but didn't say anything.

Where would she go? She had friends in London but she guessed the press would find her if she stayed in the city and she didn't want to bring this circus down around their heads. She'd given up her chance of another overseas job, wanting to stay in the UK with access to good medical facilities, through her pregnancy.

Going to her old home wasn't a possibility. Jillian, her stepmother, had made it clear that while Bess could visit for short, *very* short, stints, anything longer would be inconvenient. Bess's father, while he loved her, didn't love her enough to stand up to his wife.

Familiar pain wrapped around her heart and for a second it stole her breath. But she refused to let it overwhelm her.

She turned back to Jack, so still and watchful. Her heart beat once, twice, three times and she realised her pulse was slowing. Her earlier panic edged away. She felt safe here with him, despite all the reasons she should spurn him.

Finally, almost gently, he said again, 'So, talk to me, Elisabeth.'

Everything stilled inside her. The whirling thoughts and half-formed plans. The clamouring press wasn't important, not in the long term when her whole world had shifted and would now take a whole new course.

Now, finally, they came to it.

'I'm pregnant.'

She exhaled slowly and held his stare, feeling anew the sheer wonder of it. She hadn't told anyone else yet, had barely had time to process the news herself, but saying it aloud made it feel real.

She lifted her chin. 'With your baby.'

He nodded and surprise beat through her. She'd been prepared for disbelief and accusations that the child wasn't his. Surely pride alone would urge him not to believe the woman who'd walked out on him.

Her brow scrunched. 'You believe me? Just like that?'

Jack shrugged, those straight shoulders looking impossibly wide under tailored white linen. A tickle of heat threaded through her body but Bess ignored it. This was more important than desire. It was desire that had led her into this fix.

Except, despite the poor timing and the unexpectedness of it, she couldn't quite bring herself to think of this baby as a problem.

She'd never been baby-mad like some women. Yet she'd understood in her heart of hearts that one day she'd like children. She wanted to pass on that special love she'd shared with her mum. That was a bond she missed terribly yet still felt sometimes on the darkest days. Her mother had been a special woman and had cherished her. She'd imbued in her daughter a confidence, a caring and curiosity about the world that Bess prized. Her father's love, by comparison, didn't feel quite so profound.

Jack leaned forward in his seat, his expression intense. 'We had sex. Lots and lots of sex.' His slow, deliberate words evoked vivid memories of their week together. Those threatened to unearth the terrible longing for him that she'd buried as deep as she could. 'That can have consequences.'

Bess shook her head. He seemed so impossibly calm. 'So you'll take my word for it that the baby is yours?'

It was as if she needed to push him, prod him into argument. Anything to keep them in conflict, because conflict she could handle. She'd learnt to her cost that when it felt like they were on the same side, with the same needs and goals, this man made her far too weak.

'You came to me a virgin the first time.' His voice was low and blatantly appreciative. The ardent gleam in his eyes played on every feminine weakness and she felt that slow twist of awareness low in her body. 'You admitted you hadn't been with anyone else after you left Paris. And,' he continued before she could interrupt, 'what we shared in the Caribbean was too profound for me to believe you returned to England and instantly took up with someone else.'

She blinked. Jack had thought it profound too? The idea undercut so many assumptions. She'd assumed he'd used sex as a deliberate ploy to bind her to him and make her return to his cosy world.

'You used condoms.' Still she couldn't quite believe his readiness to accept the news.

Another shrug. The movement of those powerful shoulders tugged a thread of desire deep inside until it hummed. She made herself look away to the green space beyond the window.

'Accidents happen,' he murmured.

Bess swung around to face him again, her voice rising. 'I don't understand how you're so calm about this. You didn't want children. The few times I raised the possibility you made it clear they didn't feature in your plans.'

She knew how important Jack's plans were. He lived his life by them.

His face took on that closed look with which she was so familiar. The expression that said he didn't want to go there and she should back off. Like when she'd asked about his past and his family.

She was tired of backing off from subjects he didn't want to discuss.

'You're right, I never wanted children.' He uttered the words with devastating simplicity and she found herself rigid in her seat. 'But now there is a child. Or, all being well, there will be. You can't expect me to ignore that.'

Yet she had. Or at least she'd wondered whether his response to her news would be to ignore it.

'Do you want to keep the baby?' he asked.

Bess stiffened. She saw his gaze drop to her abdomen and looked down to discover she'd pressed her palm there in a protective gesture as old as motherhood. She was still struggling to get her head around the news of her pregnancy and grappling with the implications, but her instinctive response was obvious.

'I do.'

It would be easier to raise a child in a committed, loving relationship but life wasn't always convenient. She'd learned that when at just fifteen she'd lost her mother. She'd discovered then that life was precious and nothing, especially future opportunities, should be taken for granted.

'Good.'

Just that one word.

Bess tried and failed to read his thoughts. He sounded as enthused as if she'd told him it would be fine tomorrow for a picnic they'd planned.

Except Jack didn't do anything as low-key as picnics.

Unless it was part of the plan to entice you back into his bed.

There'd been one memorable Caribbean picnic where they'd swum and feasted on seafood and fresh fruit before Jack had made love to her so tenderly that he'd brought tears to her eyes.

She shook her head, trying to clear it and concentrate on this vital discussion. Was it pregnancy hormones that made it hard to think clearly? Or Jack, sitting so close yet still so frustratingly unreadable?

'I'm surprised you think it good news that I'm keeping

the baby. Our marriage is over and you're not interested in a child and—'

'Don't jump to conclusions. Just because I didn't want to have children doesn't mean I don't care when there's going to be a child. There's a big difference between theory and reality.'

Bess noticed he didn't argue about their marriage being over. That was a good thing, she told herself, that he accepted that.

So why didn't it feel like a positive?

'What form does this interest of yours take?' Was she being shrewish, interrogating him as if he were in the wrong? Jack wasn't her favourite person but this pregnancy wasn't his fault. It had been an accident. Yet she couldn't drop the combative attitude.

Because it helps you keep your distance.

Because, despite everything, you'd give so much for him to hold you close one last time, your head against his chest and those strong arms around you, making you feel that everything is going to turn out okay.

Bess blinked. Where had that weakness come from? Because, with her mother gone, there was no-one truly close with whom to share the excitement and fear of this moment? Even her dear cousin Freya couldn't fill that gap.

Jack leaned in, hands clasped and elbows resting on his splayed thighs. A twitch of his forehead hinted at the suspicion of a frown.

'I'm going to be a father. That's the form my interest takes.' She heard it now, an undercurrent of feeling. Something she couldn't identify yet it was real and strong. 'I intend to be there for our child, like any good father.'

'You want to be involved?'

Those straight dark eyebrows lifted as if in surprise. 'Of course. Why would you think anything else?'

'Because you never showed any interest in children before.'

Bess was proud of her even tone, as if his announcement

hadn't shocked her to the core. She'd prepared herself for so many responses to her news but had never once expected this.

'In other people's children,' he corrected. 'But this is different, isn't it, Bess?' He paused as if lingering on the taste of the name he'd used only during the throes of ecstasy.

She shivered, not from cold but from the abrupt sense of elemental connection between them. As if they were no longer in an elegant London mansion but skin to skin, heart to heart, sharing one of life's most precious mysteries.

Her heart thudded, her pulse beating more powerfully through every part of her body as if with his words and the electric blue flash she imagined she saw in his eyes, Jack had once more cast his spell over her. She reared back in her seat.

'This is our baby and I want to take care of it, raise it, love it.' He paused, his eyes narrowing. 'Surely that's understandable.'

Yet that simple statement flummoxed her. For the first time she heard Jack talk of loving someone. He'd never claimed to love her and in fact had made it clear that he didn't. He never spoke lovingly of his family and changed the subject whenever she'd tried to learn more about them. To hear him talk now about loving their child simultaneously thrilled and disappointed her.

Thrilled because she wanted her child to be loved. Disappointed that Jack should feel that way so readily, so easily when eighteen months of her trying to be the perfect wife had made no difference to his feelings for her.

She got to her feet and paced to the large window looking over the garden, fine tremors of shock running through her.

So much for assuming Jack wouldn't be interested in their child!

'That's good. That's very good.' If she said it often enough she'd convince herself. What sort of woman was she to be jealous of her unborn baby because of its claim on Jack's affections?

Suddenly the drama and trauma of the past two days overwhelmed her. She felt appallingly on edge, blinking back hot tears and swallowing down a tangled knot of emotions.

'What is it?' Jack's voice came from close behind her. 'Why are you upset?'

Bess focused on the blur of green outside. 'I don't know.' It was a relief to admit it. She hated the feeling that she needed to watch every word. 'I just feel…'

'It's been a tough time for you.'

She sensed him move closer, could almost feel the heat of his body at her back, almost feel the curve of his fingers around her arms. If she leaned back a little she knew he'd hold her. For one long, poignant moment it was all she wanted.

But Bess couldn't afford to be weak any longer. Jack had been her kryptonite for too long. She was going to be a mother and had to change her priorities, for her baby's sake.

She swung around, her gaze skidding across his face to land at a point near his chin. 'If you don't mind, I don't want to talk anymore. I know we need to.' There were a thousand unanswered questions jostling in her brain. Dozens of different scenarios, but she wasn't ready to deal with any of them, or more specifically, to deal with Jack. 'I'm just…tired right now.'

Instead of doing the business mogul thing of pressing his advantage, Jack instantly inclined his head. 'It's been a stressful day. Not just with the paparazzi, but losing your job too.'

Her head jerked up and she met his eyes. Was it a trick of the light or was that sympathy she read? Jack had never been bombastic or bad-tempered with her, but after leaving him not once but twice, and now inadvertently causing the sort of scurrilous public speculation she knew he abhorred, she'd expected to bear the brunt of his anger.

Every time she tried to guess what was going on in his head he reminded her how little she understood him. Was he furious but hiding it well? Or had he really put that behind him and moved on?

'You know about that?'

'Given the circumstances it seemed likely you wouldn't be able to work there for the moment. Besides, your friend Janusz was still apologising as you came down the stairs.'

His tone as he mentioned the other man made her skin prickle. He couldn't believe there was something between them! No, Jack would never be jealous of her. His feelings didn't run that deep. Maybe that's why he'd been so sensible in accepting the baby was his. A jealous man surely wouldn't be so trusting and reasonable.

Funny how flat that made her feel.

'We'll talk about the baby later. In the meantime there's the question of where you can go to have some respite from the press.' He paused. 'Do you have any thoughts?'

Elisabeth blinked, taken by surprise.

She'd been racking her brain for a place to go. Her flat was impossible. At the same time she'd expected him to announce he'd already arranged for her to be bundled away somewhere that suited him. Perhaps in this posh town house or an expensive hotel. Somewhere where they could continue the discussion about their child at his convenience.

'Anywhere in particular you'd feel comfortable?'

Jack was asking her for her preference? Not telling her what he'd already planned? Her forehead puckered. Had her angry words about him always taking charge sunk in?

Maybe they had.

She'd realised when she confronted him in the car about his behaviour that she'd never really done so before. Through their marriage she'd tried to be the wife he wanted, not rocking the boat. When she left it had been more important to get away than discuss what had gone wrong.

Because she'd learned to avoid conflict? After her dad remarried she'd tiptoed around his new wife, fearing that to stand up against her pettiness would force her father to choose between them. His love was inconstant. His heartbreak over her mother's death had been short-lived and his casual affection for Bess wasn't enough to make him champion her against Jillian's spite.

Bess had learned to ignore the jibes and unfriendliness so she could still see her father and Tom, her little half brother.

Had her habit of stoic silence morphed into cowardice?

You should have been frank with Jack about how you felt earlier.

As if that would mend their marriage! Jack might make a show of asking her opinion but it was still a vastly unequal match. She'd fallen in love with him while his deeper feelings weren't engaged.

At the moment she'd almost have preferred it if Jack already had a solution to where she could hide out so she didn't have to make a decision. How contrary was that?

'There aren't many places they wouldn't find me.'

'What about with your family? I know it's one of the first places they'd look but it's a large estate. Surely you could manage to keep out of sight there.'

Bess shook her head. 'That's not going to work.' She refused to go into detail about her stepmother's antipathy. 'In other circumstances I'd try Freya but not now. I don't want to drag her into this.'

Freya and Michael were back from their secret honeymoon and preparing for their official royal wedding. Bess refused to foist any negative publicity on them.

'I could find an unobtrusive hotel.'

The words were barely out when Jack shook his head. 'Don't underestimate the paparazzi. It would take just one sighting to have them camped on your doorstep. And hotel staff can be bribed. It would be okay until they found you. After that you could say goodbye to any privacy.'

His words sent a chill through her veins.

'I have a suggestion.' He paused, capturing and holding her gaze.

Bess sighed. She wasn't going back to him and their life in Paris. Not that he'd suggested that, she reminded herself. 'All reasonable suggestions are welcome.'

'I know of a house, a country house on an estate not too far out of London. You'd have complete privacy in the grounds so you could relax, undisturbed. Plus it's close enough for you to be able to reach London easily, for a doctor's appointment or whatever.'

'A house in the country?'

She'd always loved the freedom of rambling over her family's rural estate. Walking, riding, even pottering in the garden with her mother, had been therapeutic when she had things on her mind. She'd always yearned for a cosy home with rural views and had even tried to persuade Jack to live within commuting distance of the city.

'There's a village nearby but the grounds are private.'

'What about the owner?'

'Out of the country, but there are staff so you wouldn't have to do anything but rest.'

Bess regarded him curiously. How did he know about this house? Clearly it wasn't his, for Jack had always been adamant about the need to base himself in one vibrant city or another. Was it a friend's?

At this point she was so tired she didn't care. She was just grateful to have a place where she could rest and gather her thoughts while she worked out what to do next. 'That sounds marvellous, if you can arrange it for a short time.'

'Leave it to me.'

Jack's mouth curved in a hint of a satisfied smile that made her wonder abruptly if she'd just walked into a trap.

CHAPTER TEN

BESS OPENED HER eyes to a blur of green. She blinked, realising they were driving through a wood and she'd fallen asleep on the drive out of London.

Despite Jack next to her in the car!

Even dopey from sleep, she felt that familiar fizz in the air telling her that he was near.

She should have been too wired to sleep with him beside her. Too annoyed and wary. But rest had been in short supply since the Caribbean. Add to that the stress of the paparazzi.

And you're pregnant. That can make you tired.

Bess blinked, sideswiped again by the realisation. How long before the shock wore off?

A haze of blue appeared beneath the trees. She smiled. She'd always loved the bluebell woods at home, loved spring there and the way the gardens burst into life.

She swallowed, surprised to find her throat constricting. Because Moltyn Hall wasn't home anymore. Jillian preferred her not to visit and Bess's father liked to keep Jillian happy. It had been years since Bess had enjoyed spring there.

She blinked again, blaming changing hormones for the rush of emotion. Rather than sit up, she kept her face turned to the window, her cheek pressed against cushioned leather rather than face Jack. She needed to get herself under control.

The car rounded a curve and they emerged from the trees. She had no idea where they were except it was beautiful, a swathe of green dipping away from wooded hills. Water glinted at the bottom of the shallow valley and then… Her breath caught and she sat up.

Bess had grown up in an imposing old home that had been passed down through generations of aristocratic ancestors. She'd spent weekends in houses that were national treasures and in one instance, a turreted castle. But she'd never seen anything quite like this.

Sunlight danced on the square moat surrounding an old house that was a hodgepodge of warm brick with half-timbered sections. It looked Tudor in age or maybe older. With light reflecting on large mullioned windows and ornate stone carving over a massive doorway with its own footbridge, it belonged in a romantic fairy tale.

Bess stared. There were decorative chimneys, the pattern of each unique. Bright daffodils crowded the edge of the moat where a couple of swans glided. The whole place had an air of cosy charm that belied the mansion's size.

'You like it?'

Jack's voice burred over her skin, drawing it tight. But for once her physical response to him didn't bother her. She was too wrapped up in delight.

'It's remarkable,' she breathed. 'You said a house in the country. I didn't expect this.'

A moated manor house. So beautiful it made her heart squeeze. Maybe it was the tranquillity. Or the pretty, slightly overgrown garden, the perfect place to while away a summer's afternoon or for children to play hide and seek. Even the glimpses of a walled garden and an old-fashioned water mill on a small lake beyond the house added to the feeling that this was a magical place.

'You like it then? It's *good* remarkable?'

She turned, surprised that he'd asked a second time, to find him scrutinising her closely.

'Of course, good remarkable.' How could he doubt it? But

Jack's taste ran to opulent hotels where everything was perfect. This old gem was weathered and quirky. Breathtaking and no doubt incredibly expensive, but homely and endearing in a way she suspected would never appeal to him.

'It's…' She shook her head. It was the sort of place she could imagine making a home. '*This* is where I'm going to stay?'

Jack had mentioned staff but she'd imagined something smaller, more ordinary. This place spoke to her and made her wonder if he understood her better than she'd thought.

It had to be coincidence that it matched her so well. He obviously knew the owner who was happy for her to be here. It was sheer coincidence that the hideaway he'd found made her heart sing.

'Yes, the owners are away indefinitely and it's ideal. It's in the middle of a private estate and there's good security so you don't need to worry about paparazzi.'

Bess turned to the house. Naturally Jack saw privacy and seclusion, rather than the romantic beauty of the place.

That highlighted their differences. It wasn't that Jack didn't have a heart or that she wasn't practical, but she doubted he'd look at a place like this and *feel* its warmth.

The car stopped near the stone bridge across the moat. 'Come on. Let's get you settled.'

Jack stifled a smile as they crossed the bridge and entered a square courtyard, the house surrounding them on four sides. Elisabeth's eyes shone as the housekeeper welcomed them and led them on a tour.

His instinct had been right. His wife approved. The tension that had sat between his shoulder blades since Paris unravelled a little.

He remembered her showing him around Moltyn Hall, her childhood home. She'd spent little time on the remaining heirloom pieces, the valuable ones her father hadn't been able to sell. But she'd lingered lovingly in the long gallery with its

ancient, uneven wooden floor and mullioned windows looking over the rambling park. She'd grinned over the secret pas-
sages and parchment map that, according to family lore, led
to unfound treasure. She'd clearly adored the slightly unkempt
walled garden and vast grounds.

He'd only seen photos of this place but had been sure Elisabeth would like it. It had been impulsive, arranging this, but
an impulse based on close observation of his wife.

They passed through a ground-floor library and up to a
gallery where light shimmered across the ceiling, reflected
from the moat below. Elisabeth paused by a long window seat,
stroking the cushions, and Jack had an immediate image of
her curled up there with a book.

Then came another image. Elisabeth sitting there holding a
baby to her breast, her dark hair loose around her shoulders.

Jack slammed to a stop, undone.

Elisabeth was having his baby.

It didn't matter how many times he told himself, each time
it was amazing, shocking. And increasingly exciting.

But not just because of the baby. His need for Elisabeth
hadn't diminished. It should have. He was a proud man and
it made no sense that he'd yearn for a woman who'd rejected
him twice.

Yet there it was. He craved this woman. Always had, from
the moment he saw her. The idea of his child growing inside
her was, he discovered, extraordinarily arousing.

He couldn't afford to think about that now.

The housekeeper led them to a sitting room with windows
on two sides. The furniture was old, dark and slightly shabby
but comfortable as they settled to the afternoon tea laid for
them. Flames glowed in the ornately carved stone fireplace and
reflected off brass bowls filled with flowers. It felt…homely.

Jack watched his wife pour tea and hand him a slice of fruitcake. Another knot of tension in his spine untangled. He let
the unfamiliar feeling of peace wash over him.

He wasn't a man who craved peace. He was too focused on achievement, goal setting and triumphs. Always scaling the next ambitious height, working all hours to attain ever more taxing professional successes.

But there was something soothing about being here with Elisabeth, watching her so at ease, that made him forget all the things he had to do and the problems he had to solve. As if it was enough simply to *be*.

'You look…at home.' He heard the question in her tone. 'You've been here before?'

'Never.' Jack knew she was going to ask about his connection to the place and changed the subject. 'But it's good to be out of London, away from the press, don't you agree?'

He was almost sorry he'd asked when her brow twitched in a frown as she remembered the furore they'd left behind.

'Absolutely. It was horrible.'

Jack didn't want to press the point but he couldn't let her delude herself that this would pass. She needed to understand.

'You know it's not going to ease, don't you? They will keep trying to get photos, not just while you're pregnant but when the child's born too.'

She lowered her teacup. 'I'd worked that out.'

He should continue, remind her that there was one sure way to reduce the press's voracious appetite for a story—by mending their marriage. But he didn't have the heart for it. She'd been through enough today.

Jack wanted to pull her close and convince her to put her trust in him, let him deal with everything. He wanted to distract her by letting the ever-present embers of desire ignite. By seducing her until she fell into sated sleep and got the rest she needed.

He wanted…her.

The intensity of his need threatened to undo everything.

Jack put down his untouched cake and shot to his feet. He needed to get away. 'I'll leave you to get settled.'

That hadn't been his intention. He'd planned to stay. To use the time under the same roof to make her see their marriage wasn't over, could never be over given how they reacted to each other. That attraction, that compulsion, only grew stronger. Even today when she'd looked daggers at him, he'd seen what she couldn't hide. The longing, the spark of desire.

But he'd change his plans, for now.

'Wait!' She put down her own cup, frowning. 'You're leaving?'

Her eyes looked like pure antique gold from some fabled treasure.

Jack stilled. Since when had he indulged in such flights of fantasy?

'You don't want me here. You'll relax more without me.'

The words fell into resounding silence as he waited for her to deny it and admit she *did* want him.

He raked his hand through his hair.

What was he doing?

Inviting rejection? Again?

Between his parents and his wife he'd had enough of that to last several lifetimes. His skin crawled and his bunching muscles hunched his shoulders as he turned for the door.

'I thought you'd stay.' He swung around, wondering if he'd find an invitation in her eyes. Instead there was simply bemusement. 'This place was your idea...'

He had no trouble completing her words. It had been his idea and she expected him to press his advantage now he had her isolated from her home and friends.

That had been his plan.

Until his conscience intervened. It refused to let him push when she was so stressed.

Anger was metal sharp on his tongue. Anger at himself and at her.

'I have things to do. Business to see to.'

For once it was a lie. Leanne had put everything on hold,

all his meetings deferred and urgent matters delegated so he could sort out their marriage.

His wife stared, mouth compressing in disapproval as she rose. 'You can't go yet. We need to talk about the baby. *That's* the most important thing right now.'

Impatience stirred. Of course it was. Hadn't he dropped everything to be here? Yet he needed to leave. Elisabeth wasn't the only one whose world was in turmoil at the news of her pregnancy. Jack felt as if he'd spun out of control, grappling to hang on to something solid and make everything stable again. All the time the need to reach for her grew and grew, threatening his good intentions.

His control was slipping.

She stopped before him, so serious. Yet to his chagrin he couldn't help noticing the sweet curve of her parted lips and the way her breasts pressed against the taut fabric of her dress. Were those lovely breasts plumper?

Arousal was a ripple of sparks across his palms and fingertips, making him shove his hands into his pockets.

'I need to understand what you want, Jack. You said you wanted to be involved so I assume you want access.'

'Access?' The word sounded like a lawsuit.

She tilted her head as if to read his expression better. 'How *much* do you want to be involved? Occasional visits? Photos?'

He frowned. 'I don't want *access*. I'm going to be father. I intend to be there all the time.'

Her indrawn breath was a sharp hiss as the colour leached from her face. 'You expect to bring up our baby?'

Jack's frown ground into a scowl at her dismay. Did she have to be so appalled? He mightn't be a natural father but he'd work hard at it. She couldn't know his fears that he'd fail. He reminded himself that with his father's pathetic example as a warning, surely he could do better.

'That's exactly what I mean.'

But she was already shaking her head, her eyes huge in her

face. She clasped her hands together so tight it looked like she'd cut off the circulation.

'What are you going to do? Try to buy the baby from me? Or try to take it by force?'

Jack's head snapped back as if from a blow. 'Force? What are you talking about?'

She swallowed, the movement jerky. She looked physically frail yet the fire in her eyes threatened to burn him to cinders.

'You're rich and can afford the best lawyers. I don't have much by comparison.' Her chin shot high. 'But I won't let you take sole custody. No matter what, I'll find a way to stop you.'

He rocked back a step, horror solidifying in his gut and paralysing his larynx.

Finally he found his voice. 'You really believe I'd do that?' He drew air into hollow lungs. 'What have I ever done to give you such a low opinion of me?'

His chest was on fire, at odds with the cold frosting his skin.

She stared at him, eyes glazed and the pulse at the base of her neck thrumming. She blinked, black pupils huge in her fiery eyes. 'I...'

Jack stalked to the window. A pair of snow-white swans skimmed the green waters below but he barely saw them. 'You think I'm a monster?'

He spun around to find her just behind him.

She was pregnant and stressed. He tried to tell himself her accusation didn't matter, but it *did*. It felt like a cleaver striking his chest, sinking past flesh, bone and muscle right to his soul.

'I've spent my life trying to be a decent man.' A better man than his father. 'Ambitious and successful, yes. But honest and honourable.' And caring. He wanted to care for his child, though he feared he didn't know how. Was that such a crime? He grimaced. 'Why would you believe, even for a second, that I'd behave that way?'

'I'm sorry, Jack.' She shook her head, her teeth anchoring

deep on her plush lower lip. 'I don't really… I'm sorry. I pan-icked. I just feel so overwhelmed, like I've got no control.'

Her words struck home. Wasn't that how he felt? For Jack control had been his way of rising above his emotions. Emo-tions that were never returned. Emotions he'd banished from his life years ago.

Except you're feeling now, aren't you? Feeling too much.

Slowly the blurred edges of his vision cleared and he man-aged to breathe over the ache in his chest where her words had carved so deep.

'We're both adjusting to the news of the baby.' See, he could be reasonable, despite the provocation. Yet it took everything he had to suppress his outrage.

Elisabeth spread her hands. 'How exactly do you see the future, Jack?'

'It's simple. We're having a child.' He paused, holding her golden-brown gaze and feeling again that pulse of excitement. 'I want to be there, raising it, with you.' He let her absorb that. 'We're married and I want us to stay that way. Bringing up our baby together. Giving it a warm, loving environment.'

All the things he hadn't had from his own parents.

It sounded simple but he knew how rare and valuable that was. He'd do whatever it took to provide that for his child.

'That won't work. You know I want a divorce.'

Jack stared down at his wife, valiantly fighting his baser instincts. The urge to prove her wrong, prove she wanted him as much as he wanted her, was almost irresistible.

'But I don't want one.'

She stepped back. 'That's impossible. Our marriage was a disaster.'

Was. Past tense.

Jack refused to accept that.

'I disagree.' He raised his hand to stop her when she would have objected. 'We have problems but they're not insurmount-able.'

Nothing was insurmountable. He'd convince her to stay with him by force of will if nothing else. He'd worked all his life to achieve what he had. He'd fought for every success. He intended to fight for this.

'You're only saying this because you want the child.'

'*Our* child.'

'Our child.' Her eyes narrowed accusingly. 'But you can be a father without being married. You're not really interested in us as a couple. We can negotiate an arrangement for access. That would be easier on everyone.'

Jack felt the storm brewing inside him. Muscles stiffened and sinews tightened. 'I'm not interested in us as a couple?'

He took a step towards her, closing the space between them. He read her confusion and fear and something that shimmered between hope and excitement. That cut through his hard-won control. The knowledge that, despite her arguments, Elisabeth *wanted* as badly as he.

'You're wrong there. Completely wrong.'

Her eyes widened but her expression turned mulish as she crossed her arms.

'You've never been interested in our marriage as anything more than a convenient arrangement.'

His bark of laughter exploded before he could stop it. 'The joke's on me then, isn't it?' he said as he stalked closer. 'Convenient isn't the way I'd describe the last year.'

She returned his stare. 'That proves my point. Our marriage is a mess. There's nothing holding it together except the legalities.'

All day Jack had reined in his emotions. He'd been calm and understanding, not berating her for running out on him or letting him find out about their baby from the media. Not smashing even one paparazzi camera.

He'd allowed her silence and space. He'd held back and let her decide what she'd like to do and where she'd like to go rather than take charge. He'd risen above his indignation at seeing her turn to another man, letting him touch her yet shrinking away from Jack.

He'd ignored the hunger riding him so hard, the need to reach out to her, not just to reassure her but to ease the deep ache inside him.

Now his control splintered. He could cope with anything but lies. They'd littered his childhood. Broken promises about caring for him, reading bedtime stories, taking him to some event, even simply being in the house when he woke up. How many times had he counted on a promise or told himself that a casual parental hug meant they really cared, only to find himself deserted and alone for days on end?

His words emerged softly. 'Nothing holding our marriage together?' He watched her eyes flare, felt the need pulse between them. 'Then what about this?'

He bent slowly, watching her parted lips, daring her to step away and lie to him, and herself, again.

He paused, his mouth millimetres from hers.

There was a sound—a sob?—and her eyelids drifted down. That sound yanked at his heart. Despite everything she'd done he didn't want to distress her. But he refused to let her hide behind a blatant lie.

Jack cupped her cheek, fingertips sliding into her silky hair. Her sigh was a puff of warmth on his face.

When he touched his lips to hers it was as he'd known it would be. Fire and dazzle and the familiar, sudden rush of pleasure. But something deeper too. Tenderness. The world telescoping to the pair of them in this fragile moment of connection. Their mouths barely connected yet the very air felt heavy with anticipation.

Her hands landed on his chest and she leaned in, angling her head for better access. The tip of her tongue stroked his lips then his tongue, and abruptly that moment out of time dissolved into a rush of heady excitement.

Jack wrapped an arm around her waist, drawing her in,

feeling her nestle between his legs. His other hand cupped her head as he deepened the kiss.

Far from objecting, Elisabeth looped her arms around his neck, straining against him. She tasted of fruitcake and something more tantalising, something utterly feminine. Her slim frame was supple yet strong and it blew his mind to think she cradled his child inside.

That had to be why this kiss seemed different from any he'd known. Despite their rising excitement, betrayed by their increasingly urgent caresses, this felt profound rather than carnal. Like a question asked and answered. Like revelation and affirmation.

Jack breathed in the dusky rose scent of her, stroked her trembling body and kissed her with all the passion he'd held back. He bent her over his arm, holding her securely against him, uncaring that with their hips melded together his eagerness for her must be unmistakable.

Maybe her thoughts followed the same path. Elisabeth gave a sinuous wriggle and pressed against his groin, as if trying to melt their clothes with her body heat.

Her tongue danced against his, demanding then retreating, leaving him so eager and needy it would only be moments before he shed the mantle of sensible adult and took her against the closest flat surface like a gauche teenager.

His blood thickened to lava, muscles turning rigid and his caresses more demanding.

She welcomed that, sliding against him as if intent on sending him over the edge.

It would be easy to forget his good intentions. But his brain still worked enough to remind him that no matter how good they were together sexually, Elisabeth didn't trust him.

He had to win that trust. There was no other option. He refused to walk away from their marriage, and their child, in defeat.

Finally, he dragged his head up, lungs heaving like bellows

as her stunned amber eyes opened. Gently he unwrapped her hands from his neck.

'When you have time to think you'll realise our marriage is more than a legal agreement. It's *real*. And it's a perfect basis for bringing up our baby together.'

Reluctantly he stepped back. 'You've made it clear you're not ready to face that yet. So I'll leave you to think and rest. We'll talk later.'

Jack turned and made himself walk out the door.

CHAPTER ELEVEN

JACK HAD SAID he'd see her later. Bess had assumed he'd give her the night. At a stretch another day.

Not two whole weeks!

She'd made it clear she didn't want his company but hadn't expected him to take her at her word.

It annoyed her. She told herself it was because they had unresolved business. The sad truth was that she missed him.

How could that be?

Since the Caribbean he'd been constantly on her mind. More since London when he'd swept her out from under the noses of the paparazzi. She'd spent so long bemoaning the way he'd once organised her life, yet that day it had been wonderful to be rescued.

More intriguing was the way he'd deferred to her on how she'd leave and where she'd go.

As if he really had listened to her complaint about him taking charge and making plans for her. As if he wanted to change for her.

She didn't know whether to be grateful or resentful that he'd left her alone in this gorgeous place. He'd done what she wanted, giving her privacy, but it highlighted that despite everything wrong between them, she still yearned for him.

Memories of their lovemaking haunted her nights. Sometimes she'd swear she felt the stroke of his hand over her flesh, teasing her tender breasts and sending her to the edge of climax. So potent were those memories and her need.

Was he devious enough to stay away, guessing at her sexual frustration?

Bess stopped where the track opened into a glade, breathing the sweet spring scent of bluebells. It was the place she came to think. Yet still her life and her emotions were a terrible tangle.

She'd demanded a divorce yet every night when Jack phoned to see how she was, her pulse quickened. Despite her misgivings, she enjoyed his solicitousness. Worse, she was addicted to his whisky-warm voice.

Not just his voice. She still cared for him too much.

How was she supposed to move on with her life?

She'd spent two weeks here, trying to resolve her future. She didn't have a home or a job. Jack would help financially but instinctively she felt that would complicate everything.

She wanted to be free of him yet found herself imagining the future he'd painted, where they stayed married and raised their child, giving it all the love she could wish for it. A small, defiant voice whispered that Jack had proved he could change and that with time maybe he could love her after all.

No! She couldn't let herself be seduced by that fantasy again. She turned back down the path to the house, needing distraction. Like looking for an online teaching job which would allow her to avoid the paparazzi.

As she approached the house she saw a sleek blue car. At the sound of a familiar voice her pulse quickened.

Jack.

Emotions surged. Worry that he'd try to bulldoze her. Annoyance that he hadn't warned her he was coming. Guilt over the way she'd accused him of wanting to steal her child. And running beneath them all, excitement.

She'd missed him.

Was that what he'd intended in staying away so long? Was he that Machiavellian?

But he'd simply done as she asked. She couldn't blame him for the way she felt.

Annoyed with herself, she folded her arms. Her breasts, now feeling heavier and sensitive, tingled and she dropped her arms. That, and her very slight weight gain, were her only pregnancy symptoms. Bess was honest enough to suspect her mood swings had less to do with hormonal changes than the process of trying to break up with her husband.

Because part of her didn't want to.

She relegated that thought to the deepest recess in her mind, slammed a trapdoor on it, added an enormous padlock and covered it with a boulder.

Bess drew a deep breath and told herself she was ready.

She followed the sound of conversation to find him with another man, surveying a sluice gate that led from the moat to a channel and the lake beyond. Jack stood in jeans and a pale blue chambray shirt, the sleeves rolled up to reveal strong forearms dusted with dark hair that she knew was silky to the touch.

Her insides squeezed. He looked good. Better even than in a business suit or austerely formal evening clothes. Almost, but not quite, better than bare naked.

Bess watched him tug at something near the gate. The movement accentuated his strength and agility. He could have been an athlete if he hadn't become an engineer and corporate CEO.

Her mouth dried as she took in broad shoulders and those taut buttocks, perfectly outlined by faded denim.

You still want him badly.

Just because you want something doesn't mean it's good for you.

'Elisabeth.' He'd seen her and for a fleeting moment she basked in the glow of his unfettered smile. It was like walking out of a cold cellar into bright daylight. The sort of smile she'd grown addicted to as he courted her, persuading her that a marriage of convenience wasn't only sensible but desirable.

She almost envied the naïve woman she'd been, content to hope for a miraculous happy-ever-after, despite marrying a man without a romantic bone in his body.

Bess stood taller, nodding to the estate worker beside Jack. 'Is there a problem with the moat?'

Jack thanked the other man for his time then left him to approach her. 'We were discussing the logistics of draining it temporarily. There's a damp problem in some of the rooms that will become serious if left.'

She'd seen the flaking paint and smelt the musty dampness in a couple of ground-floor rooms. 'But why are you getting involved? We're here temporarily.'

He nodded, but not before she saw a flash of something, quickly hidden, on his face. The fine hairs on her body prickled.

'Aren't we?' She tried to remember what he'd said about the owners. Were they his friends? In the eighteen months they'd lived together Jack had never mentioned acquaintances owning such a unique property.

The crazy suspicion surfaced that Jack had bought the place. But that was impossible. Jack liked urban living. His life was full of city events designed to promote his business. He preferred the convenience of luxury hotels to a home of his own.

'That's right, though the owners are away indefinitely so you can stay as long as you like.' He shrugged. 'Meanwhile, what can I say? I'm an engineer and the complexities of water management here are fascinating.'

'So you're just curious, not actually getting involved?'

A slightly wistful smile appeared on his face. It made him look younger and less serious. No trace now of the corporate giant. Her heart hammered.

'It would be tempting to do some hands-on work.' He must've seen her surprise for he shrugged. 'Boardrooms lose their gloss after a while. Doing something practical holds a certain appeal.'

Surprise lifted her eyebrows. She'd never heard Jack express anything but enthusiasm for his high-octane business. Never heard him yearn for anything else.

'I'll look into what needs to be done while we're here, scope out a possible plan of works. I'm surprised the owners haven't tackled it earlier.'

Two things struck Bess. First that he said *we*. Jack intended to stay here with her. A ripple of excitement coursed down her backbone. Secondly that he had time to investigate a complex building and engineering problem. How long did he anticipate they'd stay?

After two weeks here Bess had fallen for the old place. It was beautiful and grand, an architectural and historical treasure. But it was also quirky and cosy with uneven floors, nooks and even a secret passage.

More than once she'd imagined a small child with deep blue eyes and a shock of dark hair, running along the sunny gallery. Or children playing with the antique rocking horses.

Her breath snared. That wouldn't happen, not here. Even if the house tugged on her heartstrings as the perfect place to raise a family.

Bess couldn't afford to fantasise. She should have learned her lesson. From now on there'd be no romantic dreams. She'd focus on reality.

Which meant accepting that Jack wasn't the only one who'd behaved badly. She met his gaze squarely, hesitating for a second because she hated confrontation. Though this wasn't confrontation, it would lay her open to judgement. But it had to be said.

'I have an apology to make. The day you brought me here I accused you of wanting to buy our baby, or persuade a court to give you sole custody.'

She remembered his stark horror as she'd said it. The memory pressed on her like a weight.

'It was a horrible thing to say and I had absolutely no reason to believe you'd behave like that. We have our differences...' What an understatement. 'But you've never done anything to make me think you'd stoop so low.'

Bess spread her hands, determined to be completely honest. 'I was feeling completely overwhelmed. By the pregnancy. By the paparazzi. By seeing you again. I took out my fears on you and it was unjustified. That must have hurt and I'm sorry.'

Jack's gaze meshed with hers and warmth invaded her body. It wasn't sexual. It was a more profound sensation, like he'd reached out and gently hugged her.

'Thank you, Elisabeth. That means a lot. I've always tried to be a better man than my...' He shook his head, a self-deprecating smile twisting his mouth. 'A decent man.'

A better man than whom?

His father? His mentor? Bess knew frustratingly little about his past and nothing at all about his family. He always changed the subject when she asked and she'd learned not to ask.

Jack spoke softly, in a tone you would use to gentle a half-tamed animal. 'I want what's best. For *all* of us.'

He thought it would be best for *her*, staying married?

Perhaps he really did.

During their marriage he'd given her great joy. She'd delighted in their passion, delighted in being with him and helping him achieve his goals. It was only at the end, when she realised how unbalanced their life was, that things fell apart.

She'd loved the way he always noticed her, not just the way she looked, but smaller things like when she began to tire at the end of a long evening. Then he was all solicitousness.

Their social schedule had been packed with business-related events. But he'd also surprised her with lazy mornings in bed, ordering in room service, when they didn't rise until lunchtime and she'd been languid with pleasure. He'd bought her tickets to concerts and exhibitions he knew she'd enjoy. Taken her on weekend drives out of the city. Those outings had been balm to her country-bred soul.

At those times Bess had felt truly *seen*. Seen and appreciated in a way she hadn't felt since her mother died.

Was it any wonder, after she'd felt so rejected by her father, that she'd jumped at the chance to be with someone who truly saw her? Even if he too wanted to use her for his own ends. Her father had used her to pay his debts and her husband had capitalised on her social skills and connections.

But Jack hadn't just taken. He'd given too.

Just not in the way she'd wanted. With love.

And no matter how irritating she'd eventually found it, she knew sometimes he'd been trying to protect her with his take-charge attitude. Like in London when he'd arrived with a plan for her escape from the paparazzi. And when he'd arranged this place where she could lick her wounds in private, and decide what she wanted without him here, influencing her decision.

Yet she was no closer to making that decision.

She rubbed her arms as a chill enveloped her.

'I was going in to have afternoon tea. Would you like some?'

The look Jack sent her warmed her to the core, his eyes bright as if she'd offered him the best business opportunity he'd seen in years.

That shocked her. Did her approval matter so much?

Once she'd have wondered if he simply wanted her to like him, not for any devious reason, but because they shared a real bond. Bess couldn't allow herself to believe that. Yet as he nodded and they walked over the stone bridge and into the house, her heart beat faster.

Soon they were seated in the sitting room. With a fire crackling in the hearth and bowls of bluebells and other spring flowers scenting the air it felt particularly welcoming. She told herself it had nothing to do with Jack sprawled across from her.

'Would you like some lemon shortbread?' She offered a

plate. 'Mrs Peterson is a fabulous cook.' The housekeeper seemed to make it her mission to feed her up. Bess hoped it wasn't because she still looked drawn and tired.

'Mm.' Jack nodded as he took a bite. 'These are amazing.'

'Aren't they? Nothing beats home-made.'

'I wouldn't know,' he said, reaching for more.

Bess's curiosity rose. Lots of people didn't have parents who baked. But once again it made her wonder about his childhood. She'd grown up in a grand house but remembered the simple joy of freshly baked treats.

She firmed her mouth, yanking her thoughts to the present. 'I'll go back to London soon.' Now was a good time to broach the idea of leaving, though she'd be sad to leave and still had no clear idea of where she would go. 'I have a follow-up appointment with the doctor and need to see about a scan.'

Jack nodded. 'I'll drive you.' He poured coffee and the sharp tang of it made Bess's nostrils twitch. Her stomach roiled a little and she sat further back in her seat.

'Elisabeth? What's wrong?'

Her eyes snapped to his. He looked concerned, the cafetiere held in mid-air. There it was again, the way he saw things about her no-one else did.

'Nothing.' She lifted her cup of herbal tea and inhaled its soothing aroma. But he continued to wait so she shrugged. 'I've been sensitive to strong smells lately.'

A complicated expression appeared on his face. Concern and a dash of excitement?

She grappled with the idea as Jack collected his cup and the cafetiere, disappearing through the open door.

Was Jack *excited* about the baby? Not just determined to do the right thing, but actually excited? The idea took her by surprise. Something ignited inside, becoming a small but warming glow.

Maybe she'd been wrong and it wasn't just a sense of responsibility he felt for their baby.

He returned and took the seat opposite. 'You've had morning sickness?'

'Not really.' Suddenly she felt almost shy about discussing her body's changes. Had he noticed her slight weight gain and fuller breasts? 'It's just that some smells disagree with me. You didn't have to take the coffee away.'

He waved his hand dismissively. 'It's not important.'

Unlike her comfort.

Bess told herself any caring individual would react the same and yet...

'When is your appointment?'

'It's okay. I'll make my own way. That avoids the risk of us being seen together at the obstetrician's.'

'Pardon?'

'It would play into the photographers' hands and it would seem to confirm that you're the baby's father.'

Jack's cobalt gaze bored into her. 'I am the father.'

'Of course, but...' Was he being deliberately obtuse? 'It would inflame speculation and scandal. I know how important it is to you to avoid that.'

Because it might impact on his business.

His eyes narrowed. 'You think I'm that concerned about what people think?'

'It's why you didn't want me spending time with Lara in Paris.'

'That's different. This is about *our child.* As for avoiding scandal, that horse has bolted. The world knows our marriage has had problems.' Even now he refused to admit it was virtually over. 'But I refuse to live my life to suit public opinion. I do what I believe is right.'

He held her gaze and she felt the emotion behind every word. 'And that's to support you. To look after our child.'

Something ran through her as she absorbed his words. A current of energy. A sizzle of excitement. The stunned realisation that this really mattered to him. *They* really mattered.

'Because you see it as your duty.' But as she said it Bess knew she was selling him short.

Slowly Jack shook his head, the look in his eyes catching her breath. 'There's nothing wrong with that. But I *want* to take care of you both. To be with you.'

Bess told herself they shouldn't be, but the words were like balm to her wounded soul. This was no lie. He meant it. Something brittle cracked open inside her.

'The press can print what it likes about us going to London together.'

'Even if we then divorce?'

'You think I'm worried about being made to look a fool?' Jack drew in a breath that lifted his chest. 'Some things are more important than reputation and public opinion.'

His words settled into silence, into her heart, and she felt herself weaken. When he spoke like that it was too easy to believe his priorities really had changed.

Bess put down her cup and clasped her hands. 'But you like everything planned and going the way you want. Your life is orchestrated around your business goals. More scandal would just add to the disruption. You can't want that.'

His brief smile was unexpected, as was his nonchalant shrug. 'There's a reason I'm a planner. Because life is unpredictable. I learned very early to take control of what I can because life's chaotic and you never know what's around the corner.' The grim set of his mouth, belying the smile of a moment ago, made her wonder what had taught him that lesson. 'I plan so I can be prepared to deal with any eventuality.' He paused. 'I also learned that some things I can't control.'

'You *do* care about what people think. You married me for my connections. So you could be seen with the right sort of woman in the right sort of crowd.'

Jack tilted his head to one side. 'Some saw me as a brash colonial. I wasn't naïve enough to think I'd be easily accepted, breaking into new markets where the powerbrokers are connected by blood, marriage and old privilege. Of course I wanted you with me. That doesn't mean I'll upend my life and play safe to avoid scandal.' A smile ghosted across his lips. 'Been there, done that when you left me high and dry in Paris.'

He went on before she could think of a reply. 'I *want* to take you to London. Not just to protect you from the press. I want to keep you company. And I want to be there to see our baby when you have your scan.'

How could she argue with that? She didn't want to.

She had the unsettling feeling that she didn't have Jack's measure after all. Not just because there were chunks of his past he refused to discuss, but because his character was deeper, more nuanced than she'd believed.

Some things are more important...

He was putting her and their baby ahead of his reputation and his business.

In fact, she realised, if he intended to stay here, he must have upended his schedule completely, cancelling or deferring meetings. One of the reasons they'd moved so often was that, while much of his business was done at a distance via phone or video link, Jack preferred face to face meetings on key projects. He said that personal involvement avoided pitfalls and ensured things stayed on track.

Through their marriage he might have kept things from her but Jack had never lied. His statement about wanting to be with her and their baby wasn't a lie. She knew it with a deep, abiding certainty.

And it threatened to turn everything she understood about him on its head.

CHAPTER TWELVE

JACK SAW THE grainy blob that was his child and his throat clogged. He leaned closer to the monitor as the technician explained that the foetus seemed healthy and was developing normally.

He hung on every word yet they seemed to wash over him from a distance. His pulse roared and he was so caught up in wonder it took everything he had to make sense of her words.

He looked at Elisabeth, lying between him and the monitor, her bare, slightly rounded belly cradling their child.

When she'd lifted her top and pushed the waistband of her skirt down to reveal that slight swell, he'd felt overcome. It was the first time their baby had seemed truly real, despite the extra fullness of her breasts that had distracted him more than once.

He breathed deeply, trying to master his voice to ask some important question. Then he saw the tears spiking Elisabeth's lashes, her trembling lips. Jack closed his hand around hers. 'Everything's fine. The baby's okay.'

She turned, blinking. 'I know. I'm just…'

'Me too. It's amazing.'

That was when she smiled.

It was a smile he'd remember the rest of his days. Not a smile of gratitude because he'd paid her father's debts. Not the sweet smile she bestowed when he took her to an event or an outing she particularly enjoyed. Nor the unforgettable smile that bewitched him when they made love.

This smile spoke of shared wonder and joy.

Jack realised they were truly united in this, equally stunned and excited. There was no give or take, just sharing.

In the early days of marriage he'd been conscious that she'd married him for his money. Not that you'd guess it from her behaviour, but theirs was a transactional relationship. He wasn't foolish enough to forget that. As time passed he knew she'd become fond of him, as he had of her. As for their sex life, it had been amazing, and he prided himself on the fact that they were so compatible.

Lately things had felt different. Despite her desertion, Jack was aware of a bond between them that ran deeper than a marriage certificate or money. It had nothing to do with business or convenience.

Initially that worried him, remembering the invisible link his parents had shared, trapping them in a tainted, poisonous relationship.

Elisabeth squeezed his fingers and warmth stole through him. Jack smiled at her, overwhelmed by the peace that filled him.

Whatever this was, it was as unlike his parents' relationship as an Australian summer to bleak English midwinter.

It made him feel good. It made him hope.

It made him more determined than ever to keep his marriage and his child.

An hour later they were lunching at an exclusive London hotel. Their table was secluded and the service discreet. Most importantly, it was somewhere Elisabeth liked.

Jack had brought her here around the time they married and she'd loved the food and the relative privacy. It had struck him then that, while she shone at public events and was at ease in the most glamorous settings, she didn't demand the limelight like some lovers he'd had.

Face it, she's unique. One of a kind.

No-one else has ever made you feel this way.
Made you want so much.
Made you scared you can't keep what you have.

His stomach dropped in a sharp plunge that made him queasy.

'Jack, what's wrong?'

He shook his head. 'Nothing at all. Are you enjoying your meal?'

After a long moment her lips compressed and she said tonelessly, 'Yes, thank you.'

She concentrated on cutting a minuscule portion before lifting it to her lips, not looking his way.

The difference between their shared excitement an hour ago and her withdrawal now was stark. Jack felt like he'd lost something precious and didn't know how to get it back.

He'd tried seduction but that had backfired in the Caribbean. He was trying patience but had the horrible feeling he'd fail.

Failure had haunted him as a child when he'd believed his parents' lack of interest was because of something lacking in him. As an adult he did all he could to mitigate against failure in business. But the failure of his marriage seemed suddenly too real.

'What is it, Elisabeth? What's up?'

'So it's okay for you to ask that, but not me?' She held his gaze, her eyes accusing. 'You rebuff me so often when you don't want to talk about anything private.'

Jack sat back, astounded. He thought of all the *private* moments they'd shared. The intimacies of the marriage bed. The intensity of those very private days in the Caribbean when it had seemed to him that they'd been closer than any two people on the globe. That feeling had made him believe he'd won her back. He'd been elated, planning their return to Paris.

'Rebuff?' Anger melded with confusion. This was the woman who'd left him, twice, without giving him time to persuade her to stay. 'Just because I don't share every pass-ing thought?'

His parents had been great over-sharers and there was a lot to be said for circumspection.

Something ignited in her gaze. He felt the blast of heat in his gut. 'Passing thought? You share virtually *nothing*. I wasn't trying to pry. I was concerned about you.' She shook her head. 'Is it that you don't trust me?'

'Of course not.' How could she think it?

'Of course not.' Elisabeth put her cutlery down with a clat-ter, clearly not believing him.

'It wasn't anything important.'

Liar. It was important. Your fear about how much she means to you and the impossible idea of losing her forever.

'And you wonder why our marriage failed. You won't talk to me about anything personal.'

She was accusing *him* of destroying their marriage? She'd been the one to leave.

But she wouldn't have left if she'd been happy.

Mirroring her, he put down his knife and fork. 'Okay, what do you want to talk about? Ask me a question. Anything you want to know.'

Her eyes widened, glowing more gold than amber, and he felt a buzz as if he'd downed a shot of cognac. Her approval was more heady than alcohol.

'Really?'

Jack nodded. He had nothing to hide. He'd avoided admit-ting how much he needed her because need made you vulner-able. But he'd tell her if that was what she wanted to know. It would be a chance to press his case to stay together, because despite her wariness, the current of attraction was stronger than ever between them. She couldn't deny it. Nor could she keep blindly denying that their baby's best future was with both of them.

He'd been biding his time, not wanting to pressure her.

'Tell me about your past, Jack, your childhood. I know nothing about your background except what I read in the press. Doesn't that strike you as absurd?'

'You want to know about my childhood?'

The idea sideswiped him. It was something he never discussed, part of his life he'd sealed away in a locked compartment. He'd been so sure Elisabeth would ask about their marriage or their future.

'Yes, I do.'

She regarded him steadily and Jack wondered what she saw. He was used to masking his thoughts and feelings. But this was no business negotiation. This was his wife and, he discovered, it grew increasingly difficult to keep up his guard around her. He didn't *want* to, he realised. He wanted that strong connection between them without impediments.

Once that thought would have stunned him. Now he simply recognised it and refused to let it faze him.

Jack reached for his water glass and downed it in one.

'I was born in Brisbane. Only child to parents who were only children themselves.'

'You had no cousins or aunts and uncles?' Was that sympathy? 'I can't imagine that.'

'No, I don't imagine you can.'

She'd been an only child until her father remarried and had a son, and though she seemed to have little contact these days with her immediate family, Jack knew she had a soft spot for her young half brother and her extended family was large. There were uncles, aunts and cousins scattered throughout England and Europe. She seemed on good terms with them all.

Elisabeth's warmth and ability to maintain genuine friendships had been part of what had attracted him. He'd seen it as counteracting the deficit in his own life. Genuine relationships had been in short supply and he valued that about her.

'Were you close to your parents?'

A bitter laugh hovered on his lips but reading her concern, Jack bit it back.

'Not close. My paternal grandmother raised me from an early age.'

'I see.' Her hands pleated together on the table. 'So your parents weren't able to support you? That must have been… difficult.'

Jack's lungs squeezed as if clamped in a vice. But the pain wasn't for himself. He'd put the past behind him. The pain he felt was for this caring woman, tiptoeing through this mine-field, her expression revealing her dismay. She really did have a soft heart.

Elisabeth deserved more than one line answers. She was right, she deserved the full picture. Or as much as she needed to understand where he came from. Sharing too much would only distress her and that was the last thing Jack wanted.

He covered her tightly folded hands with one of his.

'On paper my parents were perfectly able to support me. My mother didn't work and my father ran a very successful building company. They had enough money to send me to a private boarding school and for them to take luxury vacations wherever they chose.'

Not that they'd taken him. As often as not they hadn't va-cationed with each other.

He read the question in Elisabeth's eyes.

'My parents weren't reliable,' he said finally. 'Half the time they forgot I existed. They were caught up in their own affairs and I do mean affairs. Both were selfish and volatile, ruled by emotion. I have no idea whether they married for what passed for love, or whether she married him for his money and he mar-ried her for her body. From as early as I can remember they were at each other's throats.' The husky laugh did escape then. 'Literally. There was one night when I thought he'd kill her.'

Elisabeth gasped, her hands turning to clasp his. 'Was she all right?'

Jack nodded. He hadn't been going to share that particular memory but it had slipped out as he looked into her earnest gaze.

'My mother was fine, better than fine. She loved driving him to the edge until he couldn't take any more and he admitted how much he needed her. He was the same, taking other lovers too, but taunting her about it until their anger exploded into passion. It was twisted, I realised later. But as a kid I thought love between a man and a woman was as much about inflicting pain as needing each other. It definitely wasn't about fidelity or tenderness.'

'Oh, Jack. I don't know what to say.'

'There's nothing *to* say. It's over. It has been since their car crashed on the way home from a party. Neither were wearing seat belts and both had been drinking. I wouldn't be surprised if they'd been arguing too.'

'So your grandmother raised you after that.'

Jack was about to nod, then reminded himself his wife wanted the truth. She deserved it, not a glossed-over version of it.

Elisabeth was stronger than he'd given her credit for. In the early days of their relationship, especially after discovering she was a virgin, he'd vowed to protect her and it had become habit. Now he realised that if she needed protecting it wasn't from the truth.

He'd give her what she wanted, though his murky beginnings made him feel tainted. He swallowed. That didn't matter.

'From before then. I ran away to her house one night when I was six and stayed there after that, except when I was at boarding school.'

She looked horrified and her fingers tightened around his. 'Your parents were violent to you?'

'No. They'd forgotten I was even there. I'd eaten breakfast cereal for dinner and got myself bathed and ready for bed. But I'd hoped one of them would read me a bedtime story.' He should have known better but in those days he'd still hoped for some tenderness from his parents.

'That was the night I saw my mother aim a tumbler of whisky at my father's head and he tried to throttle her. I ran away to get help. Looking back on it now, they were already ripping each other's clothes off by the time I left but I didn't understand it was their idea of foreplay.'

'I don't know what to say,' she repeated. Her husky voice told him he'd wrung her tender heart.

Jack hauled air into stifled lungs and withdrew his hand. He wasn't that scared little boy now. He didn't need her concern, though it would be easy to bask in her sympathy.

'You were close to your grandmother?'

He shrugged. 'She wasn't a cosy, motherly sort of woman but she loved me in her own way.' Elisabeth clearly wanted more. 'She didn't bake cakes or read stories but she was there when I needed her. And she was always encouraging if I studied hard and got good marks, or excelled at anything like sport and debating.' Her praise had spurred him to work harder and achieve more. 'She kept me on the straight and narrow and it's because of her that I became focused on success.'

Jack paused. 'She died the year I made my first million.'

'I'm sorry. That must have been incredibly hard.'

He nodded. It had been. He'd looked forward to her approval at his achievement. It was strange how empty it had felt without someone with whom to celebrate. He'd buried his disappointment and concentrated on the next business goal and the next.

'There's not much more to say. It wasn't an ideal childhood but it made me strong.'

Elisabeth didn't look convinced. She looked…worried, and he could guess why. She was judging him on his past. His muscles tensed and his heart throbbed faster.

He leaned forward, determined to make her understand.

'You're thinking I don't come from a stable background.

Everyone talks about how important stability is for a child and how children learn their behaviour from parents.'

Jack paused, realising he was speaking too fast. Because this was vital. He made himself slow down.

'You're wondering what sort of father I'll make, given my history. But it's precisely because of that that I'll be a good father. I know about unreliable, uncaring parenting. I know how important routine is for a child, plus trust and caring. Things I didn't experience or only experienced occasionally when one of my parents was trying to prove to the other that I loved them more.'

There'd been confusing times when his mother had lavished love on him, only to ignore him when she lost interest.

The touch of gentle fingers on his clenched fist banished those memories. He saw sadness in Elisabeth's gaze and his stomach dropped.

'That's why you weren't interested in having children? Because of your family?'

Jack hesitated. If he admitted his deepest fear that at some level he might prove as callous and selfish as his parents, it would be an argument against him raising their baby. That fear had made him shy from the idea of having children. But now their baby was a reality, his determination to be a good father eclipsed everything else.

And he'd promised the truth. 'Yes. That's one of the reasons.' The other being that he'd never met a woman with whom he could imagine having a family. Until now. 'Can you blame me?'

Bess shook her head. 'It makes perfect sense.'

No wonder children hadn't figured in his plans. She looked at his clenched jaw, the pulse ticking beneath his bronzed skin and tension clear in the set of his shoulders.

Had he wondered if he'd be a poor father? That he might have inherited bad traits?

He might have read her mind for he circled back to that, voice earnest. 'I'll work to be the best father our child can have, believe me. You know how hard I can work.'

He sat straighter and the brief glimpse she'd had of a younger, more vulnerable Jack disappeared, replaced by his trademark assurance. Yet with the benefit of her new knowledge, Bess realised her husband was neither the uber confident businessman she'd known nor the lonely little boy he'd just revealed. He was a complex mix of both and much more besides.

How had she ever thought there was no more to him than the workaholic determined to achieve his goals? A sexy, confident man, a charismatic leader with a plan for everything, even her? Why had she never queried his absolute dedication to success, his need to control his world?

Why had she never guessed that behind the confidence was someone determined to make the world a safer place for himself and, she realised now, her as well?

Pain seared and she hunched over, ashamed. Jack might have avoided sharing his past but how hard had she tried to discover more? She'd built him up into a mix of fairy tale prince, the epitome of every fantasy, and uncaring villain who used her for his own ends.

'I'm sorry,' she croaked.

His eyes widened, the flesh taut across his features.

'Don't judge me on them, Bess. I'm not my fa—'

'Of course you're not like your father.'

Her voice was so husky she had to clear her throat. He must have thought she was apologising because she intended to wash her hands of him. Was it coincidence that he'd used the more intimate form of her name? It reinforced her feeling that his words came from the heart. They weren't carefully planned.

'I meant I'm sorry about the past. About how I let you down too.'

That's what she'd done, though at the time it had felt like her only option.

She'd known he'd find it tough, facing the gossip after she left. With this new knowledge she feared her actions had been a repeat of his past hurts. Maybe she could have handled things differently.

'I shouldn't have left you so abruptly.' Even if talking through their problems mightn't have resolved anything, she'd owed him that much.

Jack's expression froze, but those dark blue eyes were bright with something she couldn't name. It made her wish things were simple between them. That there was no shared past, only the possibility of a future. But she couldn't say that. Her thoughts were a tumbled mess and her emotions all over the place. It was one thing to wish everything was right between them but life was rarely so easy. Their future and their baby's future deserved careful deliberation.

But there was one thing of which she was sure. 'Whatever happens, Jack, you'll make a wonderful dad.'

That caught him by surprise. For a second he was so still it looked like he didn't breathe. Then his eyes crinkled at the corners, his mouth curling up in a smile so warm, so rare, that it was like discovering treasure.

'Thank you, Elisabeth. I already know you'll be a great mother.'

Then he knew more than she did. She wanted the best for her child and she had a fine example in her own mother yet she couldn't shake the feeling that she wasn't quite ready for motherhood.

'Excuse me madam, sir.' She looked up to see the waiter, concern etched on his brow. 'Can I bring something else?'

She looked at her barely touched plate, the food now cold.

'The food was superb.' Jack smiled at the waiter. 'I'm afraid we got distracted.'

It was like Jack to reassure the staff who would be concerned to see almost full plates return to the kitchen. The parents he'd described had been completely self-absorbed. Jack was nothing like that. For all his formidable focus and urge to succeed, he always noticed and responded to other people, regardless of their job or social status.

It was something she'd always admired. Something she'd like their child to learn from him.

He had a right to be involved in raising their child. The question was, would it be as a part-time parent, or as a full-time father and husband?

CHAPTER THIRTEEN

THEY WERE WALKING out through the luxurious hotel when a splash of colour caught Bess's eye. The window of the exclusive boutique held just one item, a dress of deep aquamarine with a single swirling line of amber curling from shoulder to hem.

It reminded her of the crystal Caribbean waters and dazzling sunsets during the week they'd spent together.

'You'd look stunning in that.'

Jack's voice was husky, and the unmistakable current of physical awareness stopped her in her tracks. Her heart quickened. Her flesh tightened, the fine hairs on her arms standing up as she read more than admiration in the blue fire of his gaze. Passion simmered there. Desire.

It spoke to the woman she'd tried so hard to bury. The one who couldn't stop wanting her husband.

'It's beautiful,' she murmured. But she wasn't thinking of the dress so much as the way she felt when Jack looked at her that way. He made her feel proud and strong, revelling in her feminine power. No-one else had made her feel out of the ordinary the way he did.

'It would be perfect for Freya and Michael's official wedding,' he murmured.

He was right. The spectacular dress would fit right in at the royal wedding of the decade.

'I'm not sure I'll go.'

'Of course you'll go. She's your best friend as well as your cousin. She's counting on you.' Jack scowled. 'Is it because of me? Because you don't want to be seen with me?'

'No. Well, partly.' She paused. 'I don't want to detract from her special day with negative press attention. If we were seen there together it would escalate the speculation about us and the baby. I know we were photographed today, but the wedding will be on a completely different scale. It will make things harder, dredging up speculation that we've reunited.'

Jack surveyed her steadily. 'Nothing will detract from the spectacle of the royal wedding. I hear from Michael that it's going to be magnificent.' He paused, his gaze skating back to the beautiful dress in the window. 'If it makes a difference, I won't go. I don't want to spoil the wedding you've been looking forward to. I know how important Freya is to you.'

Shock was a physical weight careering into Bess, making her sway. 'You'd do that for me?'

'Yes.' He kept his attention on the display. 'Why not try on the dress?'

Bess stepped closer, reached for his hand and tugged so he turned. Long fingers closed around hers and a shiver rippled up her spine. It wasn't sexual this time, or not completely. It was familiar, warm and comforting.

She realised this connection was an aspect of their relationship she'd missed. It undercut her earlier certainty that Jack only used her for his own ends and hadn't really cared. He cared about her, more than she'd given him credit for.

'Michael means a lot to you too. You can't miss his wedding.'

Jack shrugged. 'He'll understand.'

She shook her head. 'This is wrong.' She'd seen the friendship between the two men had grown into something deep and strong. Jack didn't have many close friends. Apart from Michael he seemed to have business acquaintances and beyond that the inevitable sycophants, trying to get his attention.

She recalled what he'd told her of his past, his criminally negligent parents and a grandmother whose approval seemed to hinge on success.

'You want to go and he wants you there.'

Jack turned, his gaze searing hers. 'I don't want you uncomfortable with me attending too.'

Bess stared, bewildered by what she saw in his eyes. Could it be…hurt?

Because she didn't want to be seen with him?

She accepted his help when she needed it but what did she give in return?

She thought of the strain he'd weathered when she left him and dropped out of sight. He was strong and capable but that didn't make him immune to hurt. He'd been the one left facing the gossip while she'd sheltered out of sight in her rural classrooms.

Besides, she didn't *want* him hurting. That realisation had been building for so long and had only intensified on hearing about his past.

'Freya and Michael want us both there,' she said. 'We both want to go.' She threaded her fingers through his. 'Let's go together.'

For a moment Jack didn't react, though his scrutiny seemed more intense, making her blood sing in her veins. 'Even if the press concludes we've reunited?'

Bess shrugged, ignoring the stiffness in her shoulders, anticipating the clamour and speculation. 'Let them think what they like. They will anyway. What they print doesn't matter. Our future and our baby's future is up to us.'

Strange how easy it was to be confident with Jack beside her, his grasp warm.

A slow smile spread across his face. 'My thoughts exactly. So, are you going to try on the dress?'

She shouldn't. She had no job, no income, no permanent home, and though Jack would help with support for the baby, she bought her own clothes now and anything in this boutique would be beyond her budget. Jack had arranged for her clothes to be sent on from her London flat but there was nothing there suitable for a royal wedding.

'If it's a matter of funds—'

'Thanks for the offer, but no.' She had her savings. She released his hand. 'I won't be long.'

A few weeks later Bess finished dressing for the wedding.

Instead of staying in a city centre hotel, she and Jack were in an exclusive chalet. It was built in traditional Alpine style with a gabled roof over a deep balcony. Window boxes spilled red geraniums over wooden balustrades and the interior was a mix of old-world charm and modern luxury. Beyond her window stretched a meadow dotted with flowers. Past that a wood rose steeply up a mountain that still bore snow at its peak.

It wasn't anything like the places Jack usually stayed. Had he chosen it knowing it would appeal to her? He was proving thoughtful and considerate, consulting her and going out of his way to please her.

The chalet was undeniably luxurious but with a warmth missing in the famous hotels where they'd stayed before. Bess was delighted by the touches of traditional folk art decoration and the vases of flowers that looked like they'd been plucked straight from the meadow.

This would be the perfect place for a honeymoon. Idyllic, private, and with a big bed as soft as a cloud.

Bess bit her lip. She was doing it again, imagining herself in Jack's arms.

They'd lived in England under the same roof on and off for weeks, with him disappearing occasionally for work. Far from cementing her resolution to insist on divorce, her thoughts kept straying in the opposite direction.

Was his suggestion that they stay married so crazy?

It made sense when it came to raising their child.

They'd proved they could live together and not be at each other's throats.

A hollow laugh escaped. Far from being at each other's throats, they were polite and considerate, determined not to break their truce. Jack because he wanted to prove they could work as a couple. Bess because she feared relaxing her guard might lead her to do something she'd regret, like going to his room and seducing him.

That urge had grown so strong she'd taken to locking her door at night and putting the key at the back of her wardrobe so she couldn't give in to temptation on the spur of the moment.

Would that be so bad? He's a wonderful lover and you've missed sex so much.

It wasn't just sex she'd missed—it was Jack.

If she'd really wanted, she could have indulged in an anonymous hook-up any time since their separation. But she'd never wanted any man but Jack.

That was the problem. It was still Jack she wanted.

Jack she loved.

Bess sagged against the window, palms on the deep sill. Her heart plunged frantically.

Everything had changed between them yet the essentials were the same. She'd given her heart to her husband. And the more time she spent with him the more difficult it would be to walk away again.

He'd let her into his confidence and she'd discovered he wasn't the man she'd believed. He liked to control his world but now she understood his predilection for planning and his drive to succeed were rooted in the heartbreaking instability of his past.

His determination to organise her life looked different when viewed from that perspective. Moreover he'd proved he could change. He hadn't made a single decision on her behalf since coming to her in England. Jack asked and listened. They ne-

gotiated, though they'd reached no definite conclusion about
a divorce.

Even his decision to choose a marriage of convenience was
no longer a mark against him.

Her chest ached at the twisted example of love his parents
had set, intermingling cruelty and passion. No wonder he'd
suggested a marriage of convenience. Given the awful things
he'd revealed, Jack probably didn't believe in love.

He wasn't cold-hearted. Far from it. The man she'd come
to know harboured strong emotions. And while she didn't
agree with all his actions, he didn't pretend to feelings that
weren't there.

Bess remembered her father's ostentatious grief when her
mother died. Had it been real? He'd always leaned on her
mother. Maybe that was why he'd married Jillian so quickly,
seeking another pillar to support him.

Would Jack ever need anyone? Need her?

A tap on her door made her swing around. She skimmed
her hands down her dress and lifted her chin. 'Come in.'

The door opened and her throat dried. She'd lost count of
the number of times she'd seen Jack in formal dress, yet still
he stole her breath. Her fingers tickled with the urge to smooth
her hands over his hard chest and wide shoulders under that
superbly tailored jacket.

Then her eyes locked on his and her breath snared. She'd
seen those deep blue eyes regarding her with approval, satisfaction, desire. Even tenderness. But what she read now was
different. Something that made her heart rise and her soul sing.

Bess leaned back, grasping the windowsill for support.

Jack looked at the black velvet box in his hands and when
he met her eyes again that look was gone, his expression unreadable.

Her hand went to her throat. Had she imagined it? Wishful
thinking because she'd begun to believe change was possible
in this relationship?

'I thought you might like to wear this.' His voice was diffident, as if he expected rejection. 'I thought it would suit your dress.'

Bess knew what it was as her fingers closed around the familiar case. She'd left it and the other jewellery he'd given her in Paris. Swallowing, she lifted the lid.

There it was, the gorgeous piece he'd given her on their engagement. A triple strand of lustrous pearls formed a choker necklace and at its centre, glowing like sunlight, was a huge, square cut piece of amber.

She'd loved it on sight, especially when he said he'd chosen it because it matched her eyes and the brightness of her smile. But in those final days in Paris it had taken on a different significance. For captured in the amber was a tiny winged insect, only noticeable under close scrutiny. Once Bess had realised the true nature of their marriage she looked at that beloved piece and saw it as a symbol of her gilded cage. She'd felt like some hapless creature trapped in a bright world that would surely destroy her.

'Elisabeth? Bess?'

His hand touched hers but didn't linger. Since that devastating kiss at the manor house Jack had scrupulously avoided touching her. Now she found herself longing for more.

'You called me Bess.'

Jack frowned. 'Is something wrong? You look pale. Should I call the doctor?'

She shook her head. 'No, I'm okay.' She met his gaze. 'You called me Bess, why?'

His frown deepened. 'Why not? Others do.'

That was the point. Others did but not him. Except once or twice when they'd made love and now when, she realised, he'd been worried.

'But not you. You always use my full name. Why? Because it sounds more upper-class than Bess?' After all, he'd married her for her society connections.

ANNIE WEST   161

Just as she told herself he wouldn't answer, Jack spoke.

'It's nothing to do with class. Elisabeth suits you better. It's more complex, more interesting, not the name of someone to be taken for granted.' He paused. 'More special.' A dull flush coloured his cheekbones. 'But if you don't like me using it, I'll call you Bess from now on.'

Complex. Interesting. Special. The words brought wonder and delight.

Bess read his discomfort, as if he'd revealed some shameful secret. Why? Because from the beginning he'd regarded her more highly than she'd thought?

It was a tempting idea, especially since she'd learned Jack had trained himself to keep his feelings in.

'No, don't.' She felt suddenly out of breath and stumbled a little over the words. 'Elisabeth is fine.' More than fine. 'I like that you see me as special and complex.'

He gave a gruff laugh. 'You're definitely that, and more. Much more.' The kindling look he gave her made her abruptly aware of the huge, high bed on the other side of the room.

Quickly she spoke. 'I need to finish getting ready.' She stared at the necklace. It was beautiful, an exquisite piece of craftsmanship but also something Jack had chosen if not with love, then with admiration and consideration.

Looking at it, she experienced none of the negativity she'd felt in Paris. Jack wasn't trapping her in his world. She was free to choose. They'd both made mistakes. It was time to move on from those and focus on the future.

Her smile felt shaky as she leaned towards him. 'Thanks for thinking of it. It will look terrific with the dress. Would you mind fastening it?'

It was as well the wedding was in a packed cathedral and the reception in the palace's grand public rooms. There were guests everywhere, plus Jack owed it to Michael and Freya to behave with decorum and not cause a scandal.

He and Elisabeth had already created enough stir, arriving together. Though to his joy, she'd been adamant that she wanted to attend with him.

Excitement had spiked at that. Hope that she was softening. She hadn't mentioned divorce lately.

All the more reason to be patient, even if it killed him. That didn't stop him dwelling on the idea of taking her somewhere private. A palace this size must have hundreds of beds. Even a secluded sofa would do for what he had in mind. Or a large desk.

'What an excellent idea,' a female voice said, shocking him into awareness of his surroundings.

It wasn't Elisabeth reading his mind and agreeing, more's the pity. It was the Countess Von Something-or-Other, bedecked in sapphires and smiling at Elisabeth.

Jack yanked his mind to their conversation about promoting literacy, but kept getting distracted by his wife.

His wife.

The woman carrying his baby.

Yet, despite the possessiveness both facts evoked, his feelings for her would be strong even without marriage or a child.

Elisabeth was different to any woman he'd known. Special.

He'd never spilled so much personal history to anyone, especially not such gruesome details. It was something he'd never have done before, but their relationship had deepened.

Meanwhile their compelling attraction was stronger than ever. He'd witnessed her eyes dilate and her sudden breathlessness when he got close. The way she'd looked at him in the chalet had been almost too much. Her eyes had blazed golden and inviting, making his hands shake as he'd secured her necklace.

His much-tested control grew threadbare. Not simply because she was alluring in that stunning dress. It was the change in the way she was with him. Her approval as she surveyed

him so intently. As if he'd done something to surprise her in
the best of ways.

She made him eager to prove her faith in him. He wanted
to do more than build commercial success upon commercial
success. Wanted to be more spontaneous, though for years he'd
shunned spontaneity, remembering his parents' impetuosity.

A wealthy entrepreneur approached, someone with whom
he wanted to make contact. Yet it wasn't business on Jack's
mind. 'If you'll excuse us, Countess, they're playing our tune.
Aren't they, darling?'

Elisabeth looked up, startled. Yet she didn't object when
he slid his arm around her waist and pulled her close. How
good that felt.

She murmured something to the other woman about being
in contact later and let him guide her onto the dance floor
where a waltz had started up. The entrepreneur stopped in his
tracks, frowning, but Jack had no time for him.

'*Our* tune?' Elisabeth whispered. 'I didn't know you were
a fan of Strauss.'

'Is that the composer or the conductor?'

Her gurgle of amusement at his joke rippled through him,
easing the tension that had built when he'd held himself back
from her.

'I don't remember you being so eager to dance. Usually
you're busy networking.'

Jack pulled her close, her fragile skirt wafting around his
legs. Her body aligned with his so wonderfully that for a second he forgot how to breathe. He watched her eyes widen, saw
the silent gasp on her open lips.

It had been too long for both of them.

'I was a fool,' he ground out as he wrapped her more snugly
in his embrace and led her into the dance. 'Why was I working when I could have been doing this?'

Elisabeth's chuckle was sweeter than any music even if he
saw confusion in her eyes.

He pivoted, leaning her back over his arm.

She followed his unexpected move with signature grace. But it wasn't her dance skills that thrilled him. It was her trust in him, letting herself dip back, reliant on his hold. Dazzling eyes held his steadily, that flicker of excitement enticing him.

'I want to be alone with you,' he admitted. 'I need you, Elisabeth.'

Dark lashes veiled her eyes but when she met his stare her irises had saturated to bright gold. He witnessed the quick throb of her pulse and her breath's telltale hitch.

'Yes.'

Just that. A whisper so soft he barely heard it, yet he felt it in every part of his body. She wanted him. Needed him. No matter the issues they still had to negotiate, this was real and strong.

Jack hauled her close, too close for respectability, but a man had his limits.

'How many hours does a royal reception last?'

Too many, was the answer. It was late when they reached their accommodation. Hours ago Elisabeth had begun to wilt at his side but she'd been determined to stay for the whole celebration. He'd had to grit his teeth rather than march over to Michael and insist they curtail the celebrations because Jack's pregnant wife was tired.

She swayed when they alighted from the car and he swept her up into his arms, ignoring her shocked gasp. 'I can walk.'

'But why should you when I can carry you? You're out on your feet.' He caught her gaze in the warm light spilling from the entrance. 'Let me do this for you.'

Elisabeth must have been exhausted for she nodded and rested her head against his chest. The simple gesture struck right to his heart. He told himself it wasn't proof she trusted him completely but for now it was enough. That, and the fact she'd admitted her need for him.

He took the stairs carefully, conscious of his precious burden, not wanting this interlude to end. But all too soon they reached her room. He got the door open and carried her in, depositing her gently on the snow-white eiderdown. A tumble of femininity in aquamarine silk, the most beguiling, puzzling, fascinating woman he knew.

Immediately Jack stepped back. He couldn't allow even a brief kiss. One taste and he'd need more, and despite what she'd said the ballroom, Elisabeth needed rest.

Jack drew a shuddering breath and shoved flexing hands into his pockets. 'Sleep now. I'll see you in the morning.' Without waiting for a reply he spun around and made the quickest exit of his life, before his good intentions failed.

He marched next door on stiff legs, his body rigid from a cruel mix of desire and determination. His lungs heaved like overworked bellows as he stripped his clothes off and stalked into the bathroom.

He felt only marginally in control of himself. These weeks had taught him how deep his desire for Elisabeth ran. It wasn't just physical, nor was it about her ability to help him achieve his business goals.

Jack snorted as he stepped into the vast shower. Looking back he realised that had been a convenient excuse to secure her for himself. He *had* benefited from her social skills and connections. She *had* been an asset. But that wasn't why he'd married her.

He wrenched on the cold tap and turned his head up to the rain shower, letting it pummel him from head to toe. His flesh drew tight from the icy spray yet even that couldn't immediately douse the heat burning inside.

He turned, eyes still closed, and frowned. Something was different. The skin between his shoulder blades prickled, the sensation coalescing and running as a line of heat down his backbone and around his groin. A light drift of scent caught his nostrils. Lush rose.

Jack's eyes snapped open.

There, in the open door, stood Elisabeth.

Her hair was down in a glossy tangle around her shoulders. Her slender arms and legs were bare, deep gold against the pristine white of the bathroom wall, and her hands were twisted together before her. But that hint of nervousness was at odds with the determined angle of her chin and the look in her eyes as they surveyed him from top to bottom, then slowly back up, lingering where, despite the icy shower, his arousal stirred.

She hadn't come to talk about the divorce, since she'd shed the aquamarine gown. She wore an oversized T-shirt that skimmed pebbled breasts and ended at her thighs. It looked vaguely familiar, like one he used to wear. Jack swallowed, wondering if she were bare beneath it.

'The connecting door was unlocked.' Her throaty voice made his burgeoning erection pulse.

Jack fought for something to say but before he found any words she yanked the T-shirt over her head.

He had his answer. She was naked.

CHAPTER FOURTEEN

JACK'S GAZE ABRADED her bare body, scraping away the last of her tiredness, leaving her vibrantly alive and yearning.

He looked like he wanted to devour her and everywhere his hungry stare landed her body sparked into arousal.

She was wet between the legs, just taking in his potent masculine beauty.

Their passion had always been combustible and the past weeks had tested her resolve to the limit. But it wasn't simple sex that had drawn her to him tonight. It was the admission that she could no longer keep her distance.

She loved him, had always loved him. Loved him more now since their relationship had deepened.

Jack's disclosures had given her new insight. She'd *felt* his anguish as he revealed snippets of his past and understood why he strived so hard. But he hadn't sought sympathy. His recent behaviour proved he could listen and wanted to make changes. He no longer simply took charge. Even when it came to the child he was so adamant he wanted to raise, he held back, determined they needed to come to mutual agreement. He wasn't bulldozing or organising her. He treated her as an equal.

She felt...valued.

That was the ultimate turn-on.

Their eyes met and the ground shifted beneath Bess's feet. She stumbled forward as he adjusted the water temperature and opened the glass door.

'Elisabeth.' Her name was a growl that tugged an invisible chord between her breasts and her womb.

'I want you, Jack.' It was obvious but she needed to say it, *wanted* to say it. 'Let me have you.'

His nostrils flared and he grimaced as if feeling the same intense hunger that teetered close to pain. Large hands settled on her hips and pulled her into the shower. 'You can have whatever you like, sweetheart.'

Bess shivered, so aroused that even the touch of his palms and the peppering spray of warm water were sensual overload.

Before he could blow her mind with a kiss she folded her legs to kneel and press her lips to the head of his erection.

Those muscled thighs shook and he groaned.

'Bess.' She almost didn't recognise her name in that rasp of sound.

Jack's hands cupped her head, fingers circling in a caress as if trying to soothe her despite his increasing desperation as she pleasured him.

His control eroded. The shivering of his thighs grew to a tremor, his pelvis tilted, moving in concert with her, yet still he didn't try to take the lead. *She* set the pace.

Bess looked up. Towering above her was the strongest man she knew. The cobalt glitter of his eyes pierced her heart. His pleasure was hers and she wanted to give him everything.

'Stop now,' he urged. 'Let me—'

Bess squeezed him in the way she knew would undo him. He jolted, head tipping back as he groaned again. The sound twisted across every erogenous zone as she caressed him, watching until he gave himself to her.

His cry of 'Bess, Bess, Bess…' almost sent her over the edge.

When he came back to himself he bent, scooping her up against him so she felt the thunder of his heart and the mighty rise and fall of his chest. He took her mouth in a slow, sultry kiss that made her feel they'd merged into one being.

Her heart soared and she clung tight, trembling at the friction as their bodies slid together.

Her eyes shut and her only anchor was Jack. She hadn't realised they'd moved until she felt tiles at her back. Her eyes sprang open to see him looking down at her, a taut smile curving his lips.

He insinuated his hand between them, cupping her breast then gently pinching her nipple and she cried out at the arc of heat flashing from there to her pelvis.

Jack's smile widened. 'Hold that thought.'

Then he was on his knees, hands circling her breasts before sliding down, over her thickened waist to her hips and abdomen. Any thought that he might not like her pregnant body disintegrated at the excitement on his face. He shook his head, flicking water, as he feathered his fingertips across the tiny bump of her abdomen.

'Who knew pregnancy would make you even sexier?'

His voice had dropped to that deep drawl that always undid her. Then his hands moved and it was her turn to gasp.

Seeing his dark head there, between her legs, untied the scant threads of Bess's control. And his touch... He'd taken his time in the past, been incredibly thorough in discovering what she liked. Now he used that knowledge to destroy her.

But what glorious destruction. He led her step by gilded step towards a beacon of pleasure, pausing now and then to play a little, torture her with so much delight that she shook from head to toe and wouldn't have been able to remain standing but for the wall at her back and his grip, supporting her.

She was totally at his mercy, yet at the same time imbued with a bright strength beyond anything she'd known.

Jack's eyes met hers, almost black with excitement, then with one deliberately slow caress, he tossed her over the edge.

The world turned to golden sparks. Catherine wheels of light and bright, flaming heat. Bess tumbled into ecstasy, lost until powerful arms gathered her close. A soothing voice whispered in her ear as Jack rocked her against his solid frame, reassuring.

Spent and strung out on bliss, she was limp in his arms, content to lean in, melding with him so that she lost consciousness of what was him and what was her. They were just together, as they should be.

Hours later, Bess woke in Jack's arms. Sunlight peeked around the edges of the curtains and she guessed it was late.

They hadn't slept much. They hadn't even made it out of the shower after that climax. As Jack held her tenderly in his arms, the press of his erection and the feel of his slick, hard body against hers had had an inevitable effect. Soon after they were gasping out their shared orgasm as he took her from behind, one hand cupping her baby bump, the other at her breast as she braced herself against the wall.

They'd spent the rest of the night cradled together. Now she felt too comfortable ever to move again.

'Let's cancel our return trip and stay in bed today.' Jack's husky drawl made her open her eyes to meet his hungry dark blue stare.

'Sometimes you have excellent ideas, Mr Reilly.'

His smile filled her heart. 'I'm glad you agree, Mrs Reilly.'

Bess blinked, surprised at the use of her married name. Silence descended, the reminder of their unsettled marriage shattering the moment.

She guessed from his slight frown that Jack hadn't meant to call her that. Had it just slipped out? That would be unlike the man she knew who always thought carefully before speaking or acting.

His chest rose on a deep breath and his embrace firmed. He sounded almost reluctant as he said, 'We need to talk, Elisabeth. I've been putting it off, but I can't any longer.'

The coward in her wanted to deny it and focus on the easy part of their relationship, sex. To spend the day doing anything but talking. Yet she knew from the set of his mouth he was determined and she wanted this resolved too. She nodded. 'We do.' Yet anxiety brushed the fine hairs on her body erect.

'You know I don't want to divorce, but I haven't told you why.'

Bess frowned. 'You told me. You want to be a full-time dad. You want our baby to be part of a family.'

Jack stroked her arm from shoulder to elbow, his gaze following the movement. 'That's true. I want to be the one raising this child with you. I don't want some other man ever taking that role.'

A chill scudded through her at the idea of a future where she was with any man other than Jack.

That said everything about her feelings, didn't it?

His mouth twisted. 'Amazing, isn't it, for me to insist on this when I could never even commit to a permanent home?' He met her eyes and warmth replaced the chill.

'I was so messed up I couldn't even bring myself to buy a place of my own. A place for *us*.' His caressing hand stilled. 'It sounds stupid but I had a superstitious fear of putting down roots because my childhood home was a battleground, not a sanctuary. Even when I lived with my grandmother home wasn't somewhere warm. It seemed easier not to get too attached.'

To places or people?

Bess wrapped her arms around his torso and squeezed, the way her overfull heart was squeezing. 'Jack—'

'Sorry, enough of the past. We need to talk about the future. Because I *do* want to make a home, with you and our child and maybe, if you agree, more children in future.'

The glow in his eyes did the strangest things to her breathing. He wanted more children? This didn't sound like a man making the best of an unplanned pregnancy. It sounded like a man who *wanted* family.

'That's why I arranged the country house.'

Bess pulled back in his arms, stunned. 'You want to settle there? Stop moving from city to city?'

'I can commute if need be but if I'm going to be a husband and father I have to adjust how I work. Delegate more, work smarter.' He paused. 'Besides, I *want* to spend my time with you.'

She wanted to believe it, *did* believe it. But him buying that magnificent, moated house because he'd decided it suited them was a reminder of his high-handed behaviour earlier, when he saw a need or opportunity and dealt with it, then informed her.

Even if she'd fantasised about the old house being the perfect family home.

Bess planted her hand on his chest and levered herself back as far as she could. 'You bought it?'

'I wouldn't do that without consulting you.' The warmth in his expression stilled her indignation. 'I've taken a lease with an option to buy but we both need to decide if it's right. I thought the best way to do that would be to live there, and you needed somewhere quiet.'

Jack seemed to hesitate. 'If you want the whole truth, I secured the place before our week in the Caribbean. An acquaintance wanted to sell and as he described it, I thought of you. Your appreciation of quirky, rambling old houses. Your love of the country, of bluebell woods and horses. The rambling gardens you showed me at Moltyn Hall. You looked so happy there.'

It hurt to swallow. Bess remembered when she'd showed him around her old home. He was right, the gardens were a special place for her and her mother.

Yet this was unbelievable. 'You rented it *before* our week in the Caribbean? *Before* I got pregnant?'

He inclined his head.

'But why?'

His words seemed to have run dry. Then she felt a tremor

run through his large frame. He inhaled, nostrils flaring, and she had the suspicion he was deeply uncomfortable.

Jack's expression turned sombre and her heartbeat stuttered with foreboding.

'Because I wanted you back, I needed you. That's why I arranged everything meticulously, so I could convince you to come back to me.'

'You mean seduce me.' Bess dredged up remembered outrage.

'Persuade, seduce, whatever it took.' His mouth lifted in a crooked smile that looked painful. 'I refused to consider the possibility of failure. You *had* to come back to me.'

Her stomach churned. 'Because you wanted me as your hostess. For your business.'

Jack's harsh laugh surprised her. 'That's what I told myself, just as I used that excuse when I proposed marriage. The truth was inconceivable to me then.'

'What truth? What are you talking about, Jack?'

His gaze meshed with hers and his humourless laugh died. 'That I love you.'

Bess stared, dumbfounded, trying to convince herself she'd heard the word *love* from Jack. Her heart pounded so fast she couldn't catch a breath. 'Say that again.'

Gently he pulled her nearer. 'I love you. It's taken me a couple of years to work it out.' He shook his head. 'I'm a slow learner but my excuse is that I'd never come across love before, not personally, nor really seen it up close until Michael and Freya. I didn't understand what I was experiencing. Sorry, I'm rambling.'

Jack, rambling? Because he was nervous? Bess gasped. 'You mean it.'

'Of course I mean it! You think I'd lie about that?'

Her voice was soft, stunned. 'No, you always tell the truth.'

'Except when I don't *know* the truth. I told myself I married you because it was convenient and you'd be useful, and of course because of the attraction between us.' His eyes flared brighter. 'But what I felt was deeper, inexplicably deeper. It was only when you walked out that I realised how much I felt. Even then I had trouble putting a name to it.' His mouth lifted at one corner, that self-deprecating smile dragging the air from Bess's lungs.

She goggled, her mind whirling.

'I love you, Bess. I want to spend my life with you. I was too slow to realise it and, lately, too scared to tell you in case you rejected me.'

Jack, scared? It was inconceivable. Until she forgot her own confusion and excitement and really looked at him. Despite his smile his gaze was shadowed, the corners of his mouth pinched and the pulse at the base of his throat pounded out of control.

This was no ruse to persuade her into marriage. It was real. More, he'd found the perfect home she'd love *before* her pregnancy. He'd acted because of his feelings for her, not because of their baby.

'Oh, Jack!'

Bess was too choked to say more. Everything she'd felt for so long, all the stress and hope and despair, constricted her throat. She pressed her lips to his throat where his pulse raced, her hand softening on his chest.

He murmured something against her ear. It might have been her name. She couldn't tell over the tumult of her blood.

Bess's lashes were wet when he finally pulled back enough to look down at her.

It felt like the world had spun off its axis, taking her to a bright new reality. Every sense was sharpened, all those feelings she'd tried so hard to ram down out of sight burst free. Joy. Wonder. Love.

'Are those happy tears?'

She sniffed. 'I'm not crying.'

'Of course not.' Jack tenderly swiped his thumb across her cheek. The gesture was at odds with the tumult within. Far from rejecting him, Elisabeth was nestling close, stars in her eyes, and he felt on the brink of heaven.

Exhilaration filled him. Enough, almost, to trounce the nerves that jittered in his belly.

It *couldn't* be merely pity she felt.

She *wasn't* going to push him away.

Nevertheless, his hold tightened as he pulled her to him, her heart against his.

Last night had been phenomenal, not merely for the peaks of sexual satisfaction they'd achieved, but for that profound, previously unnamed element that had added meaning and poignancy to physical intimacy.

Love. His heart welled with it.

'Are you okay, my love?'

There, he'd said it again and it felt even better this time. He'd never grow tired of admitting it, though it meant opening himself up wide to someone else.

Jack realised that he wanted nothing more than to share everything with Elisabeth. The highs and lows, the love and whatever losses the future held. With her he felt able to cope with anything. Except losing her.

'Better than okay. Much, much better.'

Her eyes glowed like antique treasure. But Jack had learned that there was no treasure in the world more precious than this woman.

She cleared her throat and his satisfaction dimmed as he saw her serious expression. 'I have a confession.'

'Go on.'

Part of him, the methodical, strategic part that scouted out every permutation of a situation and every possible solution, was instantly on alert. But mainly, despite a frisson of trepidation, Jack felt hopeful. She might have reservations about a total reconciliation but she hadn't pushed him away.

Her expression was rueful and the slight flush on her cheeks intrigued. 'I feel the same.'

'Pardon?' It couldn't be so simple.

Her gaze held his and his pulse jumped at what he saw.

'I love you.'

Jack registered the unruly thump of his heart, wondering if it interfered with his hearing. But then Elisabeth wriggled higher up his body, the slide of flesh on flesh deliciously exciting. But not nearly as thrilling as what she said next.

'I loved you right from the beginning, Jack.' Amber eyes held his, unwavering. 'That's why I married you. Not because you could bail my father out of debt after his failed schemes to keep the estate afloat. But because I loved you from that first meeting.'

Was he breathing? Jack couldn't tell. Everything seemed to have stopped. Except his body must still be functioning for he heard her go on.

'I didn't know about love at first sight. I thought it a myth. But you were so…' She shook her head. 'Perfect.'

His voice was guttural. 'I'm anything but perfect.' Look at the mistakes he'd made.

'You're right, neither of us is perfect. But you're just right for me. I fell in love with you and hoped one day you'd feel the same.' Elisabeth paused. 'But in Paris I realised I was kidding myself and—'

'That's why you left, because you thought I didn't value you.' Now so much made sense.

She nodded.

'A good thing you did.'

'Sorry?' She looked stunned.

'If you hadn't left it might have taken me even longer to get my head around my feelings. That's when I realised my life revolved around you. How much I needed you, even if I didn't have a name for it.'

After a lifetime of solitude, the constraints around Jack's heart tumbled loose. He drew a deep breath, still reeling from the fact that his feelings were returned.

'You're sure, Elisabeth?'

Any successful negotiator knew not to question a break-through, much less a victory, yet even now he couldn't bring himself to accept it.

'Absolutely sure.' She stroked his cheek and he heard the scratch of bristles against tender flesh. 'I just didn't dare admit it.' Her gaze dipped from his for a second but then she met his stare unflinchingly. 'I'd come to think of myself as unlovable and was scared to risk admitting it.'

Jack's eyebrows shot high. 'Unlovable?' *He* was the one no-one had cared about.

'My mum loved me, I know that. But after she died...' Her smile was uneven. 'When I was young I thought my dad doted on me. But after her death he only saw me as someone to be his hostess and help shoulder his burdens. Then he married Jillian. She didn't like me and he'd never stand up for me. He gave up on me.'

'She's jealous of you.'

'Jealous?'

'You're beautiful and bright. You know all about Moltyn Hall and the estate, which she doesn't. The people there like and respect you but haven't warmed to her. And you shine in any social setting.'

He remembered seeing her at an event her father had hosted. She'd been the belle of the ball, charming and welcoming, vivacious in a totally natural manner that made her stepmother's brusque formality even more obvious.

'Tom loves you too.' He'd seen how her little half brother adored her.

Elisabeth's eyes turned misty. 'I love him too, but I'm not allowed to spend much time with him.'

'Then we'll have to invite him for holidays with us, won't we?'

'Really?' She looked like he'd offered her the world.

Jack's throat thickened as he recognised anew his power to make her happy, or not. The same power she had over him.

'Absolutely. I want us to be a family, a loving family. The more the merrier.'

Her eyes danced. 'That sounds just perfect!'

For the first time in his life Jack believed life could be just that...perfect. For with Elisabeth he was complete and fulfilled.

He gathered her close and began telling her all the reasons she was the only woman in the world for him.

CHAPTER FIFTEEN

'IT'S BAD, JACK. The new prime minister is hinting at cancelling the contract, more than hinting. He's talking about foreign companies only being interested in the profits they can make—'

'That's preposterous!' Jack stalked to the window, the phone to his ear, and looked out to where the moat had been drained and specialists were inspecting the manor's foundations. He spun around and marched across his office. 'His country could never afford this project without us. Its contribution won't cover our costs. This isn't about profit for us.'

'No need to convince me.' The diplomat sounded fed up too. 'This is a charitable donation you're making. But he's grandstanding, playing a nationalist card, whipping up prejudice against foreign companies.'

'At the cost of a virtually free renewable power supply for the outlying islands?'

'We believe he wants to go ahead, but he wants to appear as a strong man, taking charge of foreign investment.'

Jack shook his head. 'And they say business is cutthroat. Save me from politics and international diplomacy.'

The other man's laugh was wry. 'It's not for the fainthearted, but the fact you actually got approval for this project in the first place is a miracle.'

It had taken several years' work and a torturous consultation process, but it had been worth it. From the day he'd started turning a profit, Jack had assigned a percentage of those profits to renewable energy schemes in areas that otherwise couldn't afford them.

This project, as well as bringing electricity to areas that had never had it, was to be an example of how such an amenity could be provided at minimal cost, while respecting the local culture and environment. It was supposed to be a model for others.

Jack raked his hand across his scalp. 'What is he demanding?'

'An executive team visit, headed by *you*. He won't deal with anyone less than the CEO. Think photo opportunities, briefings to all levels of government, site visits, a gracious show of hospitality by the PM and a general show on your part of being willing to please.'

Jack snorted. 'He's not scared I'll walk away from the project? My company is doing his country a favour.'

'He knows how much time and effort have gone into getting it this far. He's no fool. He knows what this means to you personally.'

Jack digested that. It was true. He'd been in too many places in the world where lives, particularly young lives, might have been saved had there been reliable electricity to power hospitals or pump fresh water. It was one of the reasons he'd been attracted to this industry.

'What timeline are we looking at?'

'He wants a week and he's talking about next Monday.'

Monday. The day Jack was taking Elisabeth to her next pregnancy scan. They couldn't miss that. It was too important. He'd promised to be there and he *wanted* to attend. He was excited and nervous to be sure everything was well with the baby.

Besides, he'd just got back this morning from a whirlwind series of meetings outside England. They'd discussed his schedule and decided that, rather than trying to commute more often, he'd minimise his trips away and compress them as much as possible.

He'd missed her every day and he knew, from her enthusiastic welcome, she felt the same.

'That's impossible. I can get an engineering team there by then—'

'Not good enough. He's already announced the visit. He wants *you*, Jack.'

It didn't matter, Jack told himself. He could ignore this jumped-up politician and fund a similar project elsewhere.

Except Jack had been there and seen personally how badly this was needed. One of his staff came from the region. That was how he'd learned about the dire circumstances there in the first place.

He set his jaw. 'Let me think about it.'

Tossing his phone onto the desk in disgust, he headed for the door.

Despite his anger at being dictated to by some grandstanding politician, six months ago he'd have organised the visit because this project was worth it.

But he couldn't let Elisabeth down. He'd just returned from a trip. And the scan was too important. Not just the scan, but the proof that he'd be there for her when she needed him.

She'd said only a little about how she'd felt rejected by her family but Jack knew enough about rejection to understand her fear of being unlovable ran deep.

He'd told her he loved her and tried to show her every day. He couldn't, wouldn't give her cause to think he'd put business before her ever again.

Especially when they'd organised for her half brother to visit too. How would it be if Jack took off to Asia instead of being there, not just for the scan but that too?

A shiver scudded down his spine. That was *not* the way to build the family they wanted.

He couldn't risk that, no matter what else was at stake. He'd let his wife down in the past and nothing would persuade him to do that now.

* * *

Bess looked up at Jack, his bold features lit by the afternoon sun, and relaxed into his hold.

She revelled in his embrace. It was wonderful to have him home. She'd missed him, though she'd been busy with plans for the gardens and part-time teaching.

'Are you sure nothing's wrong?' She'd found him not in his office but here by the moat, watching the survey of the building, his forehead knotted. 'Have they found some new problem with the house?'

She hoped not. She'd come to love the old place.

Dark blue eyes met hers and she felt that familiar sizzle. 'No, it's all fine. It's just work on my mind.'

'Work doesn't usually make you scowl. Besides, you were happy with the outcome of your meetings when you got home.'

Home, what a wonderful word.

Bess rested her head against his shoulder and hugged him. Together they'd make this place home. Though it wasn't bricks and mortar that made a home. It was Jack.

'I am happy. Those projects are going well.'

'But something else isn't? You want to talk about it?'

He smiled. 'Thanks for the offer, sweetheart, but no. I've made up my mind how to deal with it.'

Yet the issue clearly played on Jack's mind. An hour later she was passing his office and heard him say, 'I know it's a total disaster, but I *can't* go. I'm needed here.' He sounded so tense and angry she pulled up short. 'I know, but my hands are tied. If he cancels then so be it.'

Bess moved away, not wanting to eavesdrop.

But his words revolved in her head. *I can't go. I'm needed here.* He'd sounded tense and regretful. Whatever it was, it was important.

It must involve another trip, one Jack wasn't prepared to make, and she was grateful. She liked having him here. Liked the sense of belonging that had strengthened since they'd been honest about their feelings. The more time they spent together, planning their future and sharing the minutiae of life, cemented their bond. That meant everything to her.

Jack loved her and the world was a glorious place.

Yet she couldn't settle. His stark tone teased her. So regretful. Whatever the problem, it was significant, even if he didn't want to bother her with it.

Fortunately his PA, Leanne, who rang to ask Bess if she'd attend a charity luncheon next month, wasn't so reticent when asked.

'You mean he's scrapping the project?' Bess couldn't hide her disbelief. 'After all that work?'

'He's adamant. No matter what everyone says.'

Leanne's tone made the fine hairs at Bess's neck rise. 'What do they say?'

The PA sighed. 'That the Prime Minister won't like losing the project, though it's his fault. He'll twist things publicly to make it seem like Jack promised something he couldn't deliver, raising hopes then letting everyone down. He'll blacken the company's reputation and—'

'I get the idea.' Bess felt queasy. 'Jack hasn't said why he's refusing to go?'

Leanne paused. 'No.'

But her silence suggested she'd guessed and didn't want to say.

Bess planted her palm against her rounded abdomen, her mind working frantically.

She thought of Jack's promise to cut down on travel and delegate more. Her delight at having him with her more often. Her excitement at poring over old maps and plans of the estate with him, discussing improvements and their future here. The growing sense of them living in a glorious, golden bubble of intimacy.

Because, even knowing he loved her, she felt too insecure to share him with the outside world?

Everything stilled inside. He'd even arranged it so she didn't attend business-related functions with him now. The charity function Leanne had called about was a literacy event she'd thought would interest Bess.

Her breath snagged in her cramping chest. 'I have to go, Leanne. I'll talk to you later.'

She severed the call with a shaking hand, dropping the phone.

I can't go. I'm needed here.

Because he thought she wouldn't understand how vital this project was to him, to his company and to the many people whose lives it could change?

Because he feared she didn't trust their relationship and he had to keep proving himself?

Because he knew she'd felt spurned by her family and thought her too fragile to cope if he left her when her scan was due?

Bess dropped onto a nearby sofa.

Was she fragile? A coward even?

She thought of how much she hated confrontation, skirting around her stepmother's disapproval and never challenging her father about how he never stood up for her.

She'd left Jack, twice, without discussing the situation. The first time she'd simply said she was unhappy and the marriage wasn't working, but he'd still been unwell and not up to a proper conversation about it. The second time she'd sent him a text as she boarded the plane!

When it came to admitting her feelings for him, she hadn't, not until he had. Jack, who'd never had the security of a mother's love like her, who didn't even recognise love, had been the one to confront his emotions and tell her how he felt. He'd taken that risk, not knowing whether she'd reject him.

Whereas she'd loved Jack for years and been too scared to say it out loud.

Bess wrapped her arms around her middle and rocked back in the seat.

She'd thought their relationship perfect now. But how could it be, built on such weak foundations?

'Tough day?'

Jack looked up to see Bess in the doorway, gorgeous in a figure-skimming dress of gold. The sight of her lifted his spirits.

'You've changed.' His gruff voice betrayed the effect of her beauty in clinging silk. He cleared his throat and pushed his chair from the desk. 'Are we going somewhere?'

She shook her head and sauntered across. 'No. I just wanted to look good for you. I don't want you thinking I take you for granted.'

Jack grinned and pulled her onto his lap, remembering her enthusiastic welcome when he'd returned from his trip. 'That will never happen.'

His hand skimmed her thigh as he leaned in, inhaling the scent of roses and sexy woman unique to his wife.

'But I want to be sure, so I've planned something for us.'

He pulled back to meet her eyes. 'A surprise?' His voice dipped as his thoughts strayed to some of the sexy surprises she'd given him. Arousal tightened his jeans across his groin. 'Tell me more, sweetheart.'

Her smile was smug as she moved against his erection. 'You know, I have plans for this nice, big desk of yours.' Her smile widened as she deliberately swiped her palm across the wood, pushing a folder out of the way. Jack's pulse accelerated to frantic. 'But that's not my surprise.'

He was as turned on as a teenager. He had to gulp to get words out. 'It's not?'

'No.' The teasing glint disappeared and her expression grew serious as she twisted to face him, her palms to his chest.

'Elisabeth?' He paused, reading the gravity in her gaze. 'Bess?' Anxiety tightened his nape.

'You know I love you, Jack, don't you?'

His arms tightened around her. 'And I love you. Nothing will ever change that.'

She *couldn't* be having doubts.

'I know, my darling. You love me more than I deserve.' He felt her fingers on his lips when he went to protest. 'Sh. Let me finish. You've given everything to this relationship and that feels unequal. I realised today that I haven't met you halfway. I knew I loved you for years but was too afraid to admit it until you did.'

Was that all? 'That doesn't matter.'

'It does. I got into the habit of running from things, avoiding confrontations instead of standing up for myself. It's my fault that you think I'm not strong enough to deal with changes of plan or disappointments.'

Jack reared back. 'You're disappointed in our relationship?'

'Of course not!' She cupped his jaw and pressed a lingering kiss to his mouth. But when he went to deepen it she withdrew. 'Soon. Let me finish first.'

He nodded, confused but reassured.

'You don't have to keep proving yourself to me, Jack. I'm not going to fail you again. Which is why there's been a change of plan. Next week you're travelling to Asia. Leanne's arranging the details now for you and your team.'

Jack scowled. 'Leanne told you about that?'

'Don't be angry with her. I asked because I was worried about you.'

'There's no need. I know what I'm doing.'

Elisabeth nodded. 'Yes, you're travelling to Asia and saving that deal. It's too important, for the people there and for your company, and for *you*. I know you'd never have embarked on this if it didn't mean a lot to you.'

He was already shaking his head but she kept going. 'I'm not going to collapse in a heap because you have to go away, or because it clashes with my prenatal check, or Tom's visit.

I'm not going to sulk or think you don't love me because a crisis has cropped up.'

Her eyes shone bright and true and he felt answering heat bloom deep inside.

'I love you, Jack, and that means supporting you as well as you supporting me. It means giving as well as taking. I've changed Tom's visit, he's coming a week later.' She grinned. 'Because I'm going with you. It turns out the Prime Minister and his wife are expecting their second child. I'm sure she and I will have a lot to talk about while you and her husband are busy with business.'

Jack stared, taking in the light of triumph in her eyes and the determined set of her chin. She looked formidable and sexy and he blessed her generous soul. How could she believe for a second she was anything but strong?

'You don't have to do this, Elisabeth. I don't think you're weak or unsupportive, or—'

'Good. I intend to be the best wife I can be. Loving you and supporting you any way I can, including being there and making sure you don't lose your temper with that slimy politician.'

A surprised laugh erupted from Jack's throat.

'You have no idea how tempting that is.'

'I do, because I'd love to give him a piece of my mind, playing fast and loose with his people's well-being. Trying to turn your magnificent offer into a political football.'

She sounded so fierce, as if she'd defend him against all comers. Jack liked that, so much. His pulse quickened, knowing this fiery, feisty, sweet woman stood by him.

'You don't mind me changing your plans?'

'Not in the least. I think it's brilliant. *You're* brilliant. I can't wait to see you charm the Prime Minister into submission.' She'd do it too. 'Thank you, Elisabeth. It means everything,' his voice thickened, 'knowing you've got my back. No-one has ever done that before.'

'Then get used to it, because I always will. Just as I know you'll always be here for me.'

He nodded, momentarily lost for words.

It was easier to show her how he felt.

He stood, scooping her up off his lap and depositing her on the desk. Exultation shot through him as she opened her knees so he could step between her thighs.

'There's just one thing.'

'Hm?' Jack was focused on sliding liquid gold silk up her bare thighs.

'I know the PM wanted you there on Monday but I didn't change the prenatal scan. Which means we're not arriving until Tuesday. I didn't want him thinking he could click his fingers and have you obey. That's not the way to win his respect.'

Jack paused, hands on satiny warm flesh, and met his wife's eyes.

'I couldn't agree more. Besides,' he murmured as he leaned down to kiss her, 'some things are far more important than troublesome clients. Like our baby. Like us.'

Then he kissed her and they forgot about politicians and projects and focused on what was important, their feelings for each other.

EPILOGUE

'DEAR FRIENDS, WE ARE gathered here to celebrate the loving union of Elisabeth and Jack…'

Bess smiled at the man beside her on the secluded Caribbean beach. Jack looked scrumptious in pale trousers and a white linen shirt, cobalt eyes blazing with adoration as they met hers.

The way he cradled the baby in his arms, Alexandra Amber Reilly, made Bess's heart roll over. The sight of this powerful man, so gentle and loving with their baby, always did that.

Her husband raised one eyebrow and smiled that toe-curling smile, making her think to the night ahead. Her father and Jillian had actually offered to babysit tonight.

Heat skimmed her cheeks as she turned to the celebrant. The affirmation of their marriage vows was simple but beautiful, made more so by the presence of good friends and family. Tom, as best man, beamed from ear to ear, and seeing Michael so solicitous over a pregnant Freya brought tender memories of Bess's own pregnancy.

At the end of the ceremony Jack gathered her close and she lost herself in the warmth of his smile.

'Happy, my sweet?'

'Always. So long as I'm with you.'

'You took the words out of my mouth.'

And when they kissed she knew she was home.

* * * * *

COMING SOON!

We really hope you enjoyed reading this book. If you're looking for more romance be sure to head to the shops when new books are available on

Thursday 12th October

To see which titles are coming soon, please visit
millsandboon.co.uk/nextmonth

MILLS & BOON

MILLS & BOON®

Coming next month

PREGNANT AND STOLEN BY THE TYCOON
Maya Blake

One night. It was only meant to be one night.

Genie only realized she'd said it out loud when Seve's whole body tightened, turning even more marble-like than before.

"Why are you doing this? You don't want even want a child. You said as much when we had dinner."

His eyes glinted, his incisive gaze tracking her as she paced in the small cabin. "What I felt a few weeks ago no longer matters."

"That's absurd. Of course it does."

He gritted his teeth. "Let me rephrase. The child you're carrying—*my* child—is now my number one priority. I'm not taking my eyes off you until he or she is born."

Continue reading
PREGNANT AND STOLEN BY THE TYCOON
Maya Blake

Available next month
www.millsandboon.co.uk

Copyright © 2023 by Maya Blake

LET'S TALK

Romance

For exclusive extracts, competitions and special offers, find us online:

f MillsandBoon

𝕏 @MillsandBoon

◙ @MillsandBoonUK

♪ @MillsandBoonUK

Get in touch on 01413 063 232

For all the latest titles coming soon, visit
millsandboon.co.uk/nextmonth

MILLS & BOON

THE HEART OF ROMANCE

A ROMANCE FOR EVERY READER

MODERN
Prepare to be swept off your feet by sophisticated, sexy and seductive heroes, in some of the world's most glamourous and romantic locations, where power and passion collide.

HISTORICAL
Escape with historical heroes from time gone by. Whether your passion is for wicked Regency Rakes, muscled Vikings or rugged Highlanders, awaken the romance of the past.

MEDICAL
Set your pulse racing with dedicated, delectable doctors in the high-pressure world of medicine, where emotions run high and passion, comfort and love are the best medicine.

True Love
Celebrate true love with tender stories of heartfelt romance, from the rush of falling in love to the joy a new baby can bring, and a focus on the emotional heart of a relationship.

Desire
Indulge in secrets and scandal, intense drama and sizzling hot action with heroes who have it all: wealth, status, good looks…everything but the right woman.

HEROES
The excitement of a gripping thriller, with intense romance at its heart. Resourceful, true-to-life women and strong, fearless men face danger and desire - a killer combination!

To see which titles are coming soon, please visit

millsandboon.co.uk/nextmonth

MILLS & BOON
A ROMANCE FOR EVERY READER

- FREE delivery direct to your door
- EXCLUSIVE offers every month
- SAVE up to 30% on pre-paid subscriptions

SUBSCRIBE AND SAVE

millsandboon.co.uk/Subscribe